'I rather had the feeling you wanted me to fail.'

A lesser man would have blushed. Max Armstrong threw back his head and laughed. 'Oh, no, Dr Harris. I may not want you as a partner, but it's nothing to do with your ability as a doctor ——'

'Just my ability as a woman,' Cathy finished for him, and then flushed as he ran his eyes assessingly over her soft curves.

'Oh, no, I'm sure your ability as a woman is unquestionable. . .'

Dear Reader

We don't travel far this month, but there is compensation in welcoming back Elizabeth Harrison after a long absence — also Stella Whitelaw and Janet Ferguson. The warmth they generate between their characters is lovely, and I'm sure you'll find their romances fascinating. We also have Caroline Anderson back again after the mammoth work she put into her trilogy, moving out of the hospital setting to explore the problems encountered by a working mother in general practice. Lots of pleasurable reading!

The Editor

Caroline Anderson's nursing career was brought to an abrupt halt by a back injury, but her interest in medical things led her to work first as a medical secretary, and then after completing her teacher training as a lecturer in medical office practice to trainee medical secretaries. In addition to writing, she also runs her own business from her home in rural Suffolk, where she lives with her husband, two daughters, mother and dog.

Recent titles by the same author:

KNAVE OF HEARTS
RAW DEAL
PLAYING THE JOKER

The above three books together form a trilogy.

JUST WHAT THE DOCTOR ORDERED

BY

CAROLINE ANDERSON

MILLS & BOON LIMITED
ETON HOUSE   18–24 PARADISE ROAD
RICHMOND   SURREY   TW9 1SR

For Hilary and John,
with thanks.

First published in Great Britain 1993
by Mills & Boon Limited

© Caroline Anderson 1993

Australian copyright 1993
Philippine copyright 1993
This edition 1993

ISBN 0 263 78183 6

Set in 10 on 12 pt Linotron Times
03-9307-52392

Typeset in Great Britain by Centracet, Cambridge
Made and printed in Great Britain

CHAPTER ONE

IT WAS a typical little Cotswold town, the broad main street lined with pretty little houses and shops of pale honey-coloured stone, liberally sprinkled with tearooms and antiques shops, with here and there a timber-framed Tudor house jutting out precariously over the pavement.

Following the directions in the letter, Cathy drove past the old stone market hall with its broad open arches and then turned right over the river.

There, just where she had expected to find it, was a sprawling stone-built house with a car park beside it, and a large sign that read, 'Barton-Under-Edge Surgery'. As Cathy turned the car into the surgery car park and switched off the engine, she felt a sudden, unexpected rush of nerves.

Ridiculous! She chided herself. Either you get the job, or you don't. It's not as if you're out of work! It really doesn't matter at all. . .

But it did, because in driving through the little town she had fallen irrevocably in love, and her bruised and saddened heart had felt suddenly at home. And so it did matter, quite enormously, that she should succeed.

She swivelled the rear-view mirror round and peered at her reflection, checking that her wild tangle of red-gold hair was still confined in the rather severe bun at the nape of her neck, that the soft green shadow which so exactly matched her eyes hadn't creased, that the

5

heat of the day and the effect of her suddenly rebellious
nerves hadn't smudged her mascara or made her ridic-
ulously tip-tilted nose shine, although nothing in the
world could rid it of the hated freckles.

Her lips still bore the trace of the soft pink lipstick
she had applied earlier, and she was torn between
appearing over-casual or touching it up, risking giving
the impression of being over-glamorous. She settled
for a quick swipe and a dab with a tissue, then, wiping
her suddenly damp palms on the tissue, she stepped
out of the car and pulled on her lightweight jacket.
Drawing a deep, steadying breath, she made her way
into the surgery.

The reception area was deserted except for a few
escapee toys. She rang the bell, and, while she waited,
she picked the toys up out of habit to return them to
the box in the corner. As well as half an armful of
bricks and blocks, there was a squeaky rabbit, grubby
with much use, and a frayed old rag doll that must have
been dearly loved in her past. Cathy smoothed back
the tangled woollen hair with a wistful smile.

'Can I help you?'

The deep voice, so unexpected in the silence, made
her jump and she squashed the rabbit, making it
squeak.

'Sorry, you startled me!' she said breathlessly, and
turned, flustered, to find herself face to face with a tall,
fair-haired man. His physique was impressive, his
shoulders filling the doorway, but it was his eyes that
drew her, eyes that seen against the golden bronze of
his tan were the most astonishing blue she had
ever seen.

'I—I'm Dr Harris—I have an interview with Dr Glover at three o'clock.'

He held out his hand. 'Max Armstrong—I'm his partner.'

She hesitated, juggled the toys into one arm and extended her own hand. His handshake was firm, brief and positively electric. Startled by the sudden warmth that flooded up her arm, Cathy loosened her grip on the bricks and they cascaded to the floor again.

'If you've finished with the toys, perhaps we should put them back in the box and proceed with your interview?' he said with a laughing smile, and the smile transformed him from plain old attractive into the most devastatingly good-looking man she had ever seen. Her heart kicked against her ribs, and she frantically put it down to interview nerves.

'We're on the run this afternoon, I'm afraid,' he explained as he straightened, his hands full of blocks, and tossed them into the toy-box. 'I've been on holiday and there's a hell of a backlog as usual—here, let me help you.'

He scooped the remaining toys out of her arms, and she drew in her breath sharply as his hands brushed casually against the fullness of her breasts. Her heart jerked again, and as she looked up into those gorgeous blue eyes she could see a devil dancing in them.

'Sorry,' he murmured, but she had the distinct feeling he wasn't. Swallowing her confusion, she stooped and picked up the last of the toys and returned them to the box hastily, then followed him through a doorway to the kitchen at the back.

Her heart was still in turmoil from the look in his eyes and the unexpected touch of his hands on a body long condemned to abstinence, and so she was relieved to see that the other man in the kitchen was much older, perhaps in his fifties, a gentle, kindly looking man with crinkles round his eyes, a slight paunch and a straightforward, no-nonsense handshake.

'Dr Harris—welcome to Barton-Under-Edge. You've met Max, I take it? Sorry about the kitchen, but we're on the drag and as we'll probably be working till seven tonight we ought to grab a bite. Have you had lunch?'

'I have, thank you. And please don't apologise. I know all about eating on the run!'

'I'm sure you do. Coffee, then?'

He poured her a cup from a jug on the machine, and she sipped it gratefully while they unwrapped some pre-packed sandwiches. Her application was lying on the table, a coffee-coloured ring on it, and Dr Glover flipped it across the table to his colleague.

'Here, perhaps you could skim your eyes over that while we get to know each other.' He smiled at Cathy. 'So, Dr Harris, tell us about yourself.'

'Of course.' Lord, she hated those sorts of questions! She cleared her throat and sat up straighter. 'Well, until recently I've been working part-time in an inner-city practice, but the practice has expanded due to redevelopment, and they want a full-time partner so I've been filling in, but I didn't think I wanted to work there full-time permanently, so I thought I'd have a look and see if there was anything more suitable.'

Oh, lord, I'm gabbling, she thought, and paused for breath. Dr Armstrong looked up from her application, those blue eyes sweeping her with blatant curiosity. 'You're thirty-five? You don't look it.'

She gave him a sugary smile. 'I dye the grey.'

'Amazing, it looks so—natural. . .' He seemed to inspect her hair for a second, and then glanced back, his eyes sharp behind the friendly twinkle. 'And yet, despite your——' one eyebrow arched provocatively '—advanced years, you've only been working part-time?'

'Until recently, yes,' she confirmed.

'You do know this is a full-time post?'

'Yes, I do. I want full-time now.'

'So why not stay on where you are? Personality problems?'

Not until I met you, she wanted to say, but bit her tongue. 'I don't want to work in an inner-city practice.'

'Too much for you?' he asked, and she sensed rather than saw the sudden shift in his attitude. Gone was the friendly smile, the mild flirting, and she felt oddly threatened.

'I thought the country air and the simpler lifestyle would benefit my son. He's just started school, and frankly I'm not happy about it. I thought a country school would suit him better.'

The atmosphere chilled even further. 'Son?'

'Dr Harris has a son of five,' Dr Glover put in. 'Stephen, isn't it?' His smile was encouraging.

'That's right.'

'Just the one?' Dr Armstrong asked, and she nodded.

'Why on earth do you want to work full-time?' he asked, his voice deceptively lazy. 'Wouldn't you rather be at home tweaking the curtains and patting the cushions?'

Cathy controlled her temper with difficulty. 'As a

matter of fact I wouldn't, but even if I would I don't have the choice. If I want any kind of a lifestyle, I have to earn it.'

'Ambitious, eh?'

'No more than any other caring parent,' she said quietly.

He eyed her dispassionately. 'I would have thought you'd be more than happy to allow your husband to make all the pushy career moves. How does he feel about a move to the country — or do you support him, too?'

A long-ago sadness touched her gently. She was dimly aware of Dr Glover's sharply indrawn breath, but she ignored it. 'Not any more — Michael died three years ago. He had multiple sclerosis.'

She looked down at her hands, but not before she saw the swift shock on Dr Armstong's face.

'I'm sorry,' he said quietly, and his rich, deep voice was tinged with remorse. 'I had no idea. I haven't really had time to study the applications.'

She lifted her eyes to his, unwilling to use her late husband as a defence against Dr Armstrong's blistering interview technique. 'Please — forget it. It really doesn't matter.'

'But it does — in many ways, in fact, I think it's even worse than if you were married,' he argued, and she could see now there was no light-hearted twinkle or mocking humour. He was deadly serious. 'You'll have no back up, no emotional support — it's a hard life, demanding, the hours are long and antisocial, they don't coincide with school holidays — there are endless insurmountable problems.'

'Not entirely insurmountable,' she corrected quietly, 'and believe me, I am aware of the problems.'

'What about night duty? What about the times you'll be on duty at Christmas? What will happen to your son then?'

'Max, I'm sure Dr Harris has considered all these points before making her application. She is, after all, facing all those very problems at the moment and apparently successfully.' Dr Glover leant back in his chair, peering at his colleague over the rim of his specs. 'Her references are excellent, her current practice will be extremely sorry to lose her, and I think you're being rather harshly judgemental. She has, after all, been working in the field for some time and has a great deal to offer.'

'She's only been working part-time.'

'For six years,' Cathy replied tightly, 'and the last six months have been full-time.'

'Why didn't you just buy some nice little house somewhere with the insurance money and settle down to raising your son properly?' he asked curiously.

Cathy's temper frayed a little further. 'What insurance money?' she snapped. 'You don't expect a young, fit man of thirty to become terminally ill! We were going to take out life policies when we bought a house—we were looking for one when he was diagnosed. One of the drawbacks of knowing you're going to die is that you can't very easily *get* life insurance!' she finished sarcastically, and then let out her breath with a harsh sigh. It wouldn't do to lose her temper with him, however infuriating he might be.

She tried again. 'I'm sorry, I didn't mean to be rude, but I can't help feeling this has no bearing whatsoever on my application. I have domestic arrangements which take into account my hours, and my reasons for needing or wanting to work are entirely my own, beyond satsifying you that I am dedicated to my profession. Perhaps some questions along the lines of vocational training and current techniques might be more relevant, particularly where your patients are concerned!'

Dr Armstrong's firm, full mouth clamped shut as if he was controlling himself with difficulty. Dr Glover, glancing between them, steepled his fingers and regarded her thoughtfully over the top.

Oh, lord, she thought, I've blown it now. He's going to tell me I'm not suitable, and that will be it, and we'll have to stay in Bristol and Stephen will have to go to that awful school and——

'What do you know about gambling?' he asked her.

'Gambling?' The question was so unexpected that she faltered for a second, but then she recovered her poise and drew a calming breath. 'It can become an addiction, like alcoholism or drug-taking. The gambler finds it impossible to stop, even when losing, and the lies and secrecy and the resultant financial consequences can cause havoc in the family. Why?'

He smiled his encouragement. 'We have a gambler on our books—I just wondered how you would deal with him.'

'I'd read his notes before I did anything,' she said, shooting a sharp glance at Dr Armstrong. 'I don't believe in making snap judgements; they are often unreliable.'

'So you wouldn't say you're intuitive?' Dr Armstrong asked, and she had the crazy feeling it was a trick question.

'Not when there are other, more reliable methods of divining information — like reading the notes,' she retorted, with a speaking glance at her application. He had the grace to flush slightly, and his lips curved in a parody of a smile.

'*Touché*,' he said softly.

'So, having read the notes and established that the condition is pathological in nature and causing havoc in the family, as you so accurately put it, what would you suggest then?' Dr Glover asked.

They discussed the psychiatric aspects of the illness and the pros and cons of various approaches for a while, then moved on to talk about the clinics run in the surgery, health-care screening and preventative medicine.

Then, while Dr Armstrong went out on a call, Dr Glover showed her round the practice premises briefly before showing her to the door.

'We'll be in touch, my dear,' he said with a reassuring smile. 'And may I apologise for my colleague? He's inclined to be a little blunt. He also finds it rather difficult to come to terms with the idea that some women have to work for a living.'

He patted her hand, and her mouth curved automatically at the avuncular twinkle in his eye.

'Please don't worry,' she assured him. 'I'll wait to hear from you.'

Summoning a confident smile, she turned towards her car, just as a young lad came running up the path clutching a blood-soaked rag round his hand.

'Martin — what's the problem?' Dr Glover asked.

'Bloody band-saw — my hand slipped. It's gone up between my fingers. . .'

He swayed, and Cathy grabbed him, propping him against her and wrapping her arm firmly round his waist. 'In you come — don't worry, we'll soon have you sorted out,' she reassured automatically.

She supported him into the treatment-room off the hallway, and while Dr Glover scrubbed his hands she took away the rag and replaced it with a sterile pad. 'It's still welling slightly, but it seems to be slowing,' she told the other doctor.

He lifted off the pad, turned the hand this way and that and then smiled at the patient.

'Just a few stitches and a week or so off work, and you'll be right as rain. You were lucky, Martin.'

He swallowed. 'Doesn't feel all that lucky,' he said with a weak attempt at a laugh.

Dr Glover infiltrated it with local anaesthetic, and sorted out a couple of packets of sutures. 'Done much of this sort of thing?' he asked Cathy quietly.

'A fair bit when I was in Casualty. Friday night and Saturday morning there's a lot of soft-tissue repair work!'

Dr Glover chuckled. 'I'll let you do it while I watch. My eyesight isn't what it ought to be, and Max is out on a call. Do you mind?'

Cathy paused. She ought to be getting back for Stephen, but he was with his grandmother and they would be fine together. She smiled. 'Of course not.'

Compared with some of the injuries inflicted by bottles and knives that she had dealt with routinely, Martin's wound was child's play, and in no time she had it sutured and bandaged, and they were seeing him off armed with painkillers.

She was just getting into her car when a big Mercedes swished into the car park and Max got out.

'Good lord, what happened to you?' he asked, and she followed the direction of his eyes to see blood smeared all over the front of her jacket.

'Oh! I didn't realise — someone came in with a cut hand, and I sutured it.'

'*You* sutured it? Where was John?'

'Dr Glover? He was there, but he said his eyesight wasn't too good and you were out —— '

'There's nothing wrong with his eyesight!' Max said wryly. 'Crafty old devil. I expect he just wanted to see you in action. Did you pass?'

Cathy thought back to Dr Glover's praise when she had finished. 'I'm afraid I may well have done.'

'Afraid?' His brows quirked. 'Why should you be afraid?'

She shrugged and looked him straight in the eye. 'I rather had the feeling you wanted me to fail,' she said candidly.

A lesser man would have blushed. Max Armstrong threw back his head and laughed. It infuriated her.

'Well? Didn't you?' she persisted.

'Oh, no, Dr Harris. I may not want you as a partner, but it's nothing to do with your ability as a doctor —— '

'Just my ability as a woman,' she finished for him, and then flushed as he ran his eyes assessingly over her soft curves, lingering momentarily on the middle button of her blouse as it strained slightly against the fabric.

'Oh, no, I'm sure your ability as a woman is unquestionable,' he said softly. 'It's about you as a mother that I have my reservations.' His eyes flicked back to hers. '*Au revoir*, Dr Harris.'

'Don't you mean goodbye?' she asked sharply, stung by his criticism and disconcerted by her reaction to his lazy scrutiny.

'No — no, as you realise I'm not in favour of your appointment, but I have no illusions. We need another woman doctor, and if John wants you to join the practice he'll ask you, and guess who'll end up picking up the slack? I suppose it could be worse — at least as a widow you're unlikely to saddle us with the burden of your maternity leave.'

He touched his fingers to his temple in an insolent little salute, and strode past her into the surgery, leaving her quivering with anger and frustration.

'Well, damn you, Dr Armstrong!' she gritted, slamming the car into gear and screeching out of the car park, spraying gravel all over the front of his Mercedes. 'Arrogant pig!'

She raved for a few minutes as she threaded her way through the little town, then when she reached the outskirts she pulled over into a lay-by and poured herself a drink of ice-cold orange from a flask she had packed earlier, giving herself a good talking-to before setting course for home.

Her temper slowly cooling, she looked around her. The countryside was beautiful, softly rolling hills, a gentle patchwork of farmland stretching away as far as the eye could see, and here and there a stonebuilt farmhouse nestled in a little cluster of barns and outbuildings.

It was the same stone that was very much in evidence in the little town houses, too, of course, as well as in the grander homes in the area. She glanced across the road. Set well back on the other side behind a low stone wall sat a lovely old house, roses and clematis tangling around the upper windows, a Virginia creeper smothering the honey-coloured stone, and she gazed longingly at it for a moment before restarting the car and pulling away.

What it must be like to have roots, to buy a house and plant climbing roses and know you'd still be there to see them grow in happy profusion all the way up to the roof. Perhaps, if she got the job, she'd be able to afford to buy a little cottage — nothing like that beautiful old house, but even a terraced house would have a wall she could grow a rose up — unless Max Armstrong had his way.

It was after six when she arrived at her mother-in-law's house, and Stephen rushed to greet her, his eyes alight.

'Mummy!' he yelled. 'Come and see — we made a cake and Granny let me decorate it! See!' He grabbed her by the hand and towed her into the kitchen.

There, resplendent on a fine bone-china plate, was a ghastly puddle of chocolate smothered in sticky Smarties.

'Oh, my goodness!' she exclaimed, and winked at her mother-in-law over Stephen's head. 'What a wonderful cake!'

'Do you want a bit?'

'Yes, please, that would be lovely, darling.'

Joan Harris eyed her thoughtfully, then put the kettle on. 'Cup of tea, I think, to go with it. Stephen, why don't you go and put your pictures in Mummy's car while we wait for the kettle to boil?'

He picked up an enormous stack of colourful daubs and zoomed out of the kitchen making racing-car noises. Cathy sighed. 'Has he been all right?'

'He's been fine,' Joan assured her soothingly. 'How did you get on?'

'Oh, God knows.' Cathy shrugged expressively. 'The boss was OK, but his junior partner was arrogant and high-handed—doesn't like working mothers. He thinks I should be at home letting my husband support me——' She caught the flicker of pain on her mother-in-law's face and sighed. 'Oh, hell, Joan, I'm sorry!'

She lifted a shoulder slightly. 'It's OK, Cathy. So, you didn't get on?'

Cathy laughed shortly. 'Get on? Are you kidding? He's a womaniser, too—a real barefoot and pregnant in the kitchen guy. Macho man unlimited. Yuck.'

Joan suppressed a smile. 'What did he look like?'

'Tall, good-looking, sexy smile, come-to-bed eyes— I wanted to hit him.'

'Why? Because he made you feel like a woman again?'

Cathy flushed and looked away, remembering the feel of his hands when he took the toys from her arms. 'Rubbish! I never want to feel like that sort of woman!'

'What sort? Real? Alive? Whole? Cathy, you're still young. I know you loved Michael, but he died nearly four years ago, and in all that time you've never even been out for a drink with anyone.'

'That's not true——'

'Not a man.'

Cathy met the gentle concern in her mother-in-law's eyes, and looked away. 'I've been busy.'

'Not that busy. Any time you want to go out, you only have to ask.' She reached out and took Cathy's hand, squeezing it gently. 'Don't let life pass you by, Catherine.'

Cathy covered Joan's hand with her other one, cradling it against her cheek. 'I don't mean to, but sometimes I think it already has. I'm thirty-five, Joan. It's too late to start again.'

'Nonsense! It's never too late. Look at me!'

Joan, widowed seven years earlier, had recently started going out to the theatre with a man she had met through the Samaritans where they both worked as volunteers. Now, in what she classed as the autumn of her life, she was busy falling in love all over again. The only drawback was, she wanted everyone to be as wonderfully happy as she was—and Cathy knew it wasn't for her.

She forced a smile. 'I see you—you're wonderful. I'm delighted things are going so well for you, but my priorities have to be with Stephen at the moment. He's all I've got, Joan, and I'm afraid my love life comes a long way down the list of what matters right now.'

Just then the focus of her affection streaked back into the room, arms flailing, and dive-bombed her lap.

'I'm a helicopter gunship—ack-ack-ack-ack——'

'Hello, darling,' she said with a smile. 'Do helicopters like chocolate cake?'

'Ye-eah! Can I have a big bit?'

The letter came a week later, when Cathy had all but given up hope. She was scanning a professional journal for the vacancies when the postman came, and she stuffed the letter in her bag, sure it was a polite but firm rejection.

She opened it during a snatched coffee-break midway through her morning surgery, and almost shrieked aloud.

So Max Armstrong had been right—John Glover had overruled him, and offered her the job. The thing was, knowing who she would be working with, did she still want it?

Yes, her heart told her. It was a fresh start, away from all the memories of Michael and the heartache of his illness and subsequent death, away from the dirt and oppression of the inner city, away from the muggings and the rapes and the stabbings—but away, too, from Joan, who had been such a tremendous support through the difficult years, and away also from all her friends.

Even so, it was the right thing for them, and she rang John Glover before she could change her mind and told him she would take the post and would be confirming her decision in writing that day.

'Excellent,' he said cheerfully. 'You're just what this practice needs, my dear, and I'm delighted you've decided to join us. If there's anything we can do to help with the move, give us a yell.'

'In fact there is,' she told him. 'I'll need somewhere to live—you don't have any ideas, do you?'

'Leave it with me,' he said instantly. 'I'll put the word around.'

She thanked him, and then went and told her own senior partner that she would be leaving.

'Good,' he said without prevarication. 'You're like a plant grown under artificial light—you look as if you need a bit of fresh air and sunshine to brighten up your foliage!'

She smiled. 'I'll miss you all.'

'We'll miss you, too, Cathy, but it's the right thing for you — and for Stephen.'

It was just what she needed to hear. In her lunch-break she contacted the headmaster of the little school in Barton-Under-Edge, and he confirmed that he would have a place for Stephen as soon as they moved.

Now all she needed was an au pair. She contacted her cousin in Paris, discovered that she had a friend whose daughter had just left school and was looking for a job in England but didn't want to work in a town, and that evening she spoke to the young lady in question on the phone.

Delphine's English was sketchy but adequate, and she sounded charming and very sensible. Immensely reassured, Cathy phoned her mother-in-law and broke the news.

'Fantastic. I knew you'd get it. Now all you have to do is charm that lovely man with the come-to-bed eyes——'

'I can't tell you anything,' Cathy said with a laugh, but secretly she was worrying about Max's attitude towards her.

Would his prejudices make him impossible to work with? Oh, well, she thought with a shrug, all she had to do was prove him wrong. That shouldn't be so difficult.

The one remaining problem was accommodation, and that was solved almost immediately as well.

She had a phone call the following day, from the only estate agent in the town, to say he had a charming little place to rent in Barton-Under-Edge, a three-bedroomed stable flat attached to Barton Manor, the impressive seventeenth-century stone-built house she had noticed on the outskirts of the town.

It sounded delightful, the rent seemed extremely reasonable, and she made arrangements to view it at the weekend.

The agent showed her round as the owner was unavailable, and it was, as she had supposed, absolutely charming. Attached to the side of the house, it was over the original stable block, now converted to a workshop and garage, and was accessed by a lovely old cast-iron staircase up the outside. A magnificent climbing rose was trained against the wall and reached almost to the eaves, and huge trusses of heavily scented apricot blooms cascaded over the doorway, drenching her with their exquisite fragrance.

The view over the rolling hills from the top of the steps was breathtaking, and, if that alone wasn't enough to convince her, the flat itself, comfortably furnished and homely, was absolutely perfect for their requirements. Her natural prudence made her check all the terms, and, that done to her satisfaction, she agreed to take it and the agent said he would send her a contract to sign.

So it was that, two weeks later and a week before she was due to start her new job, she and Stephen packed up their things, rented a van and uprooted themselves from Bristol. As she closed the front door of their old flat behind her, it was as if she had closed a door on that part of her life. Her emotions ambivalent, but hope predominating, she bolstered herself with the memory of their new home. Surely there, in those wonderful surroundings, things would start to look up.

Joan came with them to help unload, because although there was no furniture there was still a phenomenal number of boxes, and she was glad of the other woman's company.

They collected the key from the agent and Cathy drove up to the side of the house, parking at the foot of the steps.

'What a beautiful house!' Joan breathed, clearly awed.

'Isn't it? Come and see the flat. You'll love it. Stephen, come with us, please.'

'Oh, Mummy, do I have to? There's a duck with her babies!'

And there was, waddling across the grass beside the stable block, head held proudly erect, followed by an untidy line of fluffy little ducklings.

Cathy relented. 'All right, but don't go anywhere else. I don't want you wandering off!'

She led Joan up to the flat and they let themselves in, to find the place freshly polished and gleaming, a bowl of the apricot roses set in the middle of the dining table.

'Oh, Cathy, how delightful!' Joan exclaimed. 'Oh, I just know you'll be happy here!'

She hugged her mother-in-law and friend. 'I hope so — oh, Joan, I hope so. I'll find Stephen — I want to show him his bedroom. I'll have to ask the owner if we can have an area for him to play in. He'll love that. He's hated not having a garden in Bristol.'

Her heart singing, she ran lightly down the cast-iron

steps — and slap into a solid and very masculine chest.

'You!' the man exclaimed, and, with a sinking feeling, Cathy looked up into the astonished blue eyes of Max Armstrong.

CHAPTER TWO

CATHY stepped back, snatched a calming breath and dredged up a smile. 'Dr Armstrong! What a surprise.'

Goodness, she had forgotten how blue those eyes were. They glittered like sapphires—especially when, like now, they were clearly angry!

'Is this young man anything to do with you?'

Belatedly Cathy noticed Stephen, lurking uncomfortably behind Max. 'Yes—I wondered where he'd got to. He was watching the ducks——'

'Well, you should keep a closer eye on him. I nearly had to fish him out of the pond!'

'I was just following the baby ducks,' he mumbled miserably.

'Oh, Stephen! I told you not to go anywhere. You can't just do what you want, it isn't our garden. Wait until I've sorted something out, OK?'

He scuffed his toe against the gravel and nodded, evidently subdued. Apparently he had already been given a severe talking-to. She glanced up, and her attention was snagged again by the glittering sapphire chips of Max Armstrong's eyes.

'Did you want to see me?' she asked.

'I rather thought you must be looking for me.' He glanced around. 'You must have parked on the road— or did you walk?'

She laughed. 'From Bristol? Hardly—I drove the van.'

25

His eyes were riveted on hers in what seemed to be horror. 'You're the new tenant?'

'Yes — I haven't met the owner yet, he wasn't available when I looked round. Why? Do you know him?'

'You might say that,' he said drily, and groaned under his breath. 'I'll bet it was John.'

Cathy felt she was several conversations behind him. 'John?'

'Come on, Dr Harris, stop playing innocent. You know damn well who the owner is — I expect John put you up to it. He probably even told you when I was on call so you could arrange to view it when I'd be out of the way.'

Cathy's confidence faltered as his words registered in her befuddled brain. 'You — you're the *owner*?'

He sketched a tiny, mocking bow. 'That's right — and you, I gather, are my tenant. How dreadfully cosy.'

She was stunned. The place absolutely reeked of wealth. It couldn't possibly belong to him. . .

'I didn't realise that country practices were quite so financially buoyant,' she said bluntly.

'They aren't,' he replied, equally bluntly. 'So now tell me John Glover had nothing to do with this.'

A tell-tale flush crawled up her cheeks, and he nodded. 'I knew it — interfering old goat. Dammit, he really has gone too far this time.'

'I didn't know it was you, or I wouldn't have taken it,' she said frankly, 'but don't worry, I won't trouble you. Believe me, Dr Armstrong, I have no more wish to be in your company than you apparently have to be in mine. I can assure you we won't get in your way again. Stephen, go inside, please, and stay with Granny. Excuse me.' She waited pointedly until he moved out of her way, then wrenched open the back of the van and hauled out a box.

He got in her way again. 'Where are you going with that?' he asked sharply.

'My flat,' she snapped back.

"Oh, no, you don't,' he told her, his voice like flint.

Surely he didn't mean to stop her moving in? For a moment her confidence failed, but then she remembered the papers she had signed.

She lifted her chin. 'I'm afraid I *do*. I have a contract, legally binding on both of us. Excuse me.'

'No.' He took the box from her. 'It's heavy; you shouldn't be lifting this on your own.'

'Yes, well, unfortunately I don't have the luxury of a pet gorilla to do the heavy work — and anyway, how the hell do you think it got into the van?'

The strain of the move, the upheaval and uncertainty, and then on top of it all the man's unfriendliness were suddenly too much for her. She felt the hot sting of tears behind her lids, and turned quickly away before he could see.

She was too slow, however, and a second later his fingers snaked out and caught her chin, turning her back to face him.

'Tsk-tsk. Not tears — really, you should have outgrown that childish little trick by now, Dr Harris. It really doesn't work —— '

'Damn you, leave me alone!' she gritted, and, gripping his wrist, she wrenched his hand away from her face. 'I really don't need any more from you in the way of criticism and condemnation. I may not have any control over the fact that I am a mere woman, but I don't have to stand here and listen to you insulting me without any justification——'

She whirled away, furious with him and with herself for the scalding tears that splashed over and ran down her cheeks. She clamped her fingers over her mouth to trap the sob which threatened to rise and complete her humiliation, and then, quite unexpectedly, his hand came down, warm and firm and reassuring on her shoulder.

'Catherine, I'm sorry,' he said softly. 'You're right, I was way out of line and I apologise.' He gave a rueful chuckle. 'At the risk of sounding like a chauvinist, why don't you go and make a cup of tea while I bring this lot up?'

She should have enjoyed her victory, but she was too tired to care. 'The kettle's in the van,' she said wearily.

'There's one in the flat—and tea and coffee and milk. Agnes put some in this morning. Go on, you've obviously had enough, and I could do with a cup myself. I'm sure you'll make it better than me.'

'Patronising oaf,' she muttered under her breath.

'Stubborn, mule-headed feminist,' he shot back. 'Tell me this, if you hurt your back humping all this lot upstairs, who is it who'll have to cover your sick leave?'

'I don't have a bad back,' she replied with a return of her old fire, 'and for your information I haven't had a day off for myself in five years!'

'Yet,' he muttered provocatively.

She was just turning back for another go at him when Joan appeared at the top of the steps.

'Cathy, have you——? Oh! Company—and help. How wonderful!'

She clattered delicately down the cast-iron stairs and paused just above him, her curiosity barely in check. 'I'm Joan Harris, Cathy's mother-in-law.'

Max juggled the box to his left arm and held out his hand. 'Max Armstrong.'

Joan's smile broadened into one of real warmth. She came down the last steps and shook his hand firmly. 'Dr Armstrong — Max. I've heard so much about you. How kind of you to come and help. Cathy's had so much to do, and she was working right up to last night. I don't think she's had a wink of sleep, but she never complains. It is good of you to offer to carry the boxes upstairs for her.'

Cathy groaned under her breath. She could almost hear the violins!

Or was it the sound of Max's smothered laughter?

'My pleasure, Mrs Harris,' he said with a smile that was almost civilised.

Joan shot Cathy a keen look. 'I've got an idea — why don't you go upstairs and tell Max where to put everything, and I'll try and sort things out logically in the van — oh, and you could make a pot of tea while you're up there — I could just murder a cup!' and Cathy, comprehensively outmanoeuvred by a pair of masters, grumbled up the stairs and put the kettle on.

By the time the tea was brewed the van was nearly empty, and the three bedrooms and the little sitting-room were piled high with seemingly endless boxes.

As for Max, he was almost charming, and Joan, despite her advancing years still an excellent judge of what she described as 'horseflesh', declared him later to be absolutely perfect.

'I couldn't have made him better for you myself,' she

said as Cathy and Stephen left her house the following day. 'He's just what the doctor ordered!'

'In which case, it's time the little men in white coats came and took the good doctor away,' Cathy said laughingly, then, with an affectionate hug and kiss, she slid behind the wheel of her little car and set off for Barton-Under-Edge.

They had spent the night with Joan in Bristol having returned the van, and were going to spend the day unpacking before Stephen started school the following day, and Cathy was using her final week's holiday to settle them in and do a bit of homemaking—the last chance she would have before she started her new job.

Delphine, the au pair, arrived on Tuesday, by which time everything was unpacked and ready.

She was a delightful girl, and Cathy, much to her relief, liked her on sight. So, more importantly, did Stephen, and as he was also settling in well at his new school it was with a light heart and in a thoroughly optimistic frame of mind that Cathy set off for work the following Monday morning.

Considering that they were living on top of each other, Max had maintained a remarkably low profile during the previous week; apart from a visit from Stan the gardener, to tell her that she and Stephen could feel free to use the area of garden beyond the stables, and Agnes the housekeeper popping in to ask if there was anything she could do, they had had no contact with their landlord, and Cathy was beginning to think that renting his flat wouldn't be so bad as she had first feared.

Working with him, however, would be a totally different kettle of fish, she was certain. Still, she was on firm ground there, and not even he could shake her confidence in her ability as a doctor.

Her first patient, however, was less enthusiastic.

A well-dressed, athletic-looking man in his early thirties, he walked into the room, took one look at her and stopped in his tracks.

'Oh.'

She glanced down at the notes. 'Mr Carver? Do come in. I'm Dr Harris. Take a seat.'

He hesitated, and then with a resigned sigh he lowered himself into the chair she had positioned beside the desk, and gave her a wary smile.

'I wasn't expecting a woman,' he offered.

She grinned. 'That's equality for you. For years women have expected their doctors to be men. For some reason men find it uncomfortable when the boot's on the other foot, but don't worry, the most important thing is that I'm a doctor. Now, what can I do for you?'

He paused for a second, then took a deep breath and met her eyes. He was quite clearly worried. He had been fitted in as an emergency, and her list being the lightest on her first morning, he had been sent to her.

'What's wrong, Mr Carver?' she prompted gently.

He dropped his eyes to his hands. 'I think I might have testicular cancer.'

So that was it. She set down her pen and leant back in her chair. 'What makes you think that?'

He let his breath out on a sigh. 'I saw the nurse a few months ago—she runs a well-person clinic. She gave me a leaflet on self-examination, and I've been doing it regularly ever since. My brother thought I was crazy, but it's so simple—I just do it in the shower while I'm washing. Anyway yesterday I noticed a slight tenderness, and I think I can feel a sort of bump — nothing much, but I thought it would be a good idea to have it checked.' He twisted his wedding-ring distractedly. 'I haven't told my wife. We haven't got any children yet although just recently we've been leaving it to chance, but if I have got — I mean, the treatment — there won't be any children, will there?'

She smiled. 'I think you're jumping the gun here, but let's assume I find a lump that looks suspicious. The first step then is to refer you to a specialist at the hospital. They'll examine you and do an ultrasound to make sure that it's not just a cyst or a hydrocele, and if they're satisfied that it's a tumour they'll remove only the affected testicle. Now, if you've been checking yourself regularly as you say, then this will have been caught in the very early stages, and the likelihood of it having spread is very small, but speed is the important thing.'

He didn't look reassured. 'And the prognosis?'

'The success rate for this type of cancer now is between ninety and ninety-eight per cent, depending on the speed with which it's picked up and the type of cancer. And it still has to be proved to *be* cancer. It could be orchitis, or an inflammation of the membrane around the testicle — almost anything. The lump may not even exist except in your fears.'

'Oh, it exists,' he said hollowly. 'I checked yesterday because it started hurting on Friday. I played squash, and I thought I'd strained it or something, but it got worse over the weekend.'

'I think I should have a look before we go any further. Just slip your things off and lie down on the couch. I'll be with you in a minute.'

She drew the screens round him and wrote down his symptoms in the notes, then, pulling on a pair of gloves, she went behind the screen and examined him.

Her examination finished, she stripped off her gloves and left him to dress.

He emerged while she was writing up his notes and perched stiffly on the edge of the chair, his hands fisted on his knees, clearly tense.

'Well?' he asked after a moment.

She set down the pen. 'You've got a lump, I'll give you that. It's very small, but it's there.'

He looked searchingly at her. 'And?' he prompted.

'I'm going to refer you to a specialist. I'll phone him, and you should get an appointment within a matter of days. If you don't, ring me. And don't worry. If it is cancer, you've detected it very early. The operation should be very straightforward.'

'And afterwards?'

'After the operation, depending on the type of tumour and the existence of any secondaries, you'll either be given chemotherapy, which has made great strides, or radiotherapy, or a combination of both. As far as fertility is concerned it will affect the other testicle temporarily. After about two years, however, it will probably have recovered enough for you to father children. However, for insurance against the unlikely event of permanent sterility in the other testicle, you will probably be advised to store semen in a sperm bank.'

'Before the operation?'

She nodded.

'But won't it be affected? I mean, isn't there a danger it will give the baby cancer?'

She shook her head firmly. 'No, absolutely not. Hundreds of men have been treated in this way now, and many of them have successfully fathered perfectly normal children both before and after the operation.'

He was still silent, watchful. An intelligent man, he wanted the answers to all the questions. He met her eyes candidly.

'What if they have to remove both testicles?' he asked quietly. 'I mean, it's castration, isn't it?'

'It's highly unlikely that they'd need to remove both,' she assured him. 'Removal of one makes absolutely no difference to your potency, so you needn't fear that you would lose any of your masculine characteristics. Your voice, body hair and so on will remain completely unaffected. Once you've healed after the operation, you life will proceed exactly as before. That's on the medical side. On the cosmetic side, if you wish they can give you a silicon implant to replace the missing testicle. No one would ever know the difference.'

He nodded and stood up, framing a polite social smile. 'Thank you, Dr Harris,' he said calmly. As he turned away, she saw the fear still lurking behind his eyes. Cathy took the bull by the horns.

'Mr Carver, you still don't know if you have cancer. If you have, it's in the very early stages. Your chances are excellent.'

He paused at the door. 'Will I be treated any quicker if I go privately?'

'I very much doubt it. I think you'll find you see someone in a day or two. Why? Have you got private health insurance?'

He shook his head. 'We haven't got round to it. I've

got life insurance, though, although I must say I never thought I'd need it.'

She gave him a wry smile. 'I think it's extremely unlikely that you *will* need it, at least for a good many years.'

He answered with a grim smile of his own. 'Let's hope you're right. And thank you for your help.'

'You're welcome.'

He left her, and for the next couple of hours she was swept along by the tide of patients that followed.

It took her longer than usual to deal with them because she had to get used to a new computer system, but finally she reached the bottom of the heap of notes, and with a sigh she went out into the kitchen at the back, from where a delicious smell of coffee was drifting.

Max was sprawled at the table, one foot across the other knee, a cup of coffee propped on his belt buckle.

'Well, well — you've finally finished your surgery.'

She flushed under the implied criticism. 'I'm sorry I took so long, but the computer doesn't seem to like me.'

John Glover came in behind her and chuckled. 'Join the club. It has me for breakfast every day. The only person it seems to like is Max, and he can get it to turn circles on the ceiling. Oh, and Andrea, of course — the practice manager. But then she could charm the birds out of the trees.'

Cathy disagreed, but she had the sense to do so silently. She had met the coldly efficient practice manager that morning, and had taken an instant dislike to her — a dislike that was apparently mutual.

'So, how did it go?' Dr Glover asked, settling himself

down with a cup of coffee and dunking a chocolate biscuit in it.

She looked away. She couldn't afford the luxury of biscuits. She had enough trouble with her figure without eating between meals.

'OK. I had a patient this morning who thinks he's got testicular cancer, and I have to say I think he's probably right. He's the right age — early thirties — and all his symptoms fit.'

'Did you examine him?'

'Yes — there's no doubt, he's definitely got a little lump.'

'Who was it?' Max asked, idly stirring his coffee.

'Samuel Carver——'

'Sam? You're kidding!' He shot upright, slopping his coffee on the table. 'I played squash with him on Friday night, and he didn't say anything then.'

'He didn't know then. It started to hurt after he played, so he checked himself yesterday. He got the leaflet from the practice nurse a few months ago and he's been doing it regularly.'

'Bloody hell.' Max sank back against the chair, his face pale, and drew patterns absently in the pool of coffee. 'So what did you tell him? Perhaps I'd better give him a ring and put his mind at rest about the treatment.'

'I've done that. He knows exactly what will happen to him and what to expect,' she informed him a trifle tartly. How dared he imply that she would have sent a patient away without sufficient information and reassurance?

'I think I'll ring him anyway. Was he frightened?'

She eyed him closely. 'No more than you would be.'

He laughed without humour. 'Don't worry, I'd be petrified. I know it's illogical, but it's the Big C, isn't it? We're all afraid of it, even though we ought to know better, and even though it kills far fewer people than heart disease, for instance. And that, in its own way, is much more insidious. Poor old Sam. Do you want me to ring the urologist?'

'I think I can manage,' she told him drily. 'Perhaps you could give me the name of the man I want?'

'Sure. Andrea'll give you the number. It's a guy called Hart.' He unravelled his legs and stood up, stretching lazily like a big cat. 'I'll catch you both later. I'm going out on my calls now.'

She watched him leave, her temper still severely provoked by his implications.

'Ignore him,' John Glover said quietly. 'He's only baiting you. Your predecessor didn't make herself over-popular, and I'm afraid you're being judged in the same jaundiced light.'

'I thought there was something,' Cathy said wryly. 'What did she do—apart from being born a woman?'

He grinned. 'Pauline joined as a single woman in her late thirties, moved in with a friend of Max's and promptly got pregnant. Far from doing the decent thing and leaving, she had the cheek to take maternity leave and come back, very much on her own terms, and she nearly drove Max insane. Every time the baby had a cold, she took the day off. Her mind was never on the job, she didn't follow up properly—oh, she was just generally sloppy. In Max's eyes that's totally unforgivable. When she got pregnant for the second time, I thought he was going to leave, but in the end her partner got moved to another part of the country and she went with him. Good riddance, too, but she was one on her own. A blind man on a galloping horse can see you're an entirely different kettle of fish, but it'll be an uphill struggle to convince Max of that. Of course, the worst thing is he blames himself because he introduced them to each other!'

John Glover's pleasant, homely face creased with unholy laughter. 'I don't think he'll ever forgive himself for that mistake!'

Cathy smiled. 'Well, you don't have to worry about me, Dr Glover. My days of romance are over. I've settled into middle age with a sigh of relief, and all I want to do is raise my son and get on with my job.'

Her remark was greeted by a snort of derision. Glancing up, her eyes collided with the brilliant blue of Max's sardonic scrutiny.

'Commendable but unlikely,' he said drily. 'But in order to aid you in your ambition, I thought this map might help you find your way round when you go out on call.'

He dropped a folded map of the town and surrounding area on the table and left again, radiating contempt.

Dr Glover's eyebrows shot up. 'He's really got a burr under the saddle over you, hasn't he? How's the flat working out? Seen much of each other?'

'None—thankfully. I think you could fairly say that we're avoiding each other.'

He sighed. 'I'm sorry you don't get on. I was hoping that once you got to know each other—I know he seems a bit of a bigot, but he's a good bloke really. Filthy rich, of course—old money, as they say. Lovely house.'

'Yes—yes, it is. Which reminds me, when you said

you'd find out about accommodation for me, did you know that estate agent had Max's flat on his books?'

Dr Glover's eyes twinkled. 'Rumbled, am I? The estate agent happens to be a friend of mine. I told him to let the other properties slip from his mind if you asked.'

Cathy was astonished. 'But why?'

He shrugged, looking a little embarrassed. 'He's lonely, you're a pretty girl — I know you make all these noises about middle age, but you're still a young woman, Cathy. A little light-hearted romance would do you both the world of good.'

She glared at him. 'I don't believe it! I thought Max was exaggerating, but let me assure you, Dr Glover, I neither want nor need a little light-hearted romance! And if I did, the very last person I would choose would be Max Armstrong!'

She leapt to her feet and marched out of the door — slap into Max's chest.

Hot colour flooded her cheeks, and she glared at him. 'Did you hear?'

'I did — and I can't tell you how relieved I am to hear it. It circumvents all manner of problems.'

She remembered the last thing she had said, and her colour rose again. 'Not that — he fixed the estate agent!'

'I told you he had something to do with it. Why do you think he appointed you? He acts like a bloody fairy godmother — but don't worry, Catherine. You're safe. I have no intention of breaching your defences, although your assertion about middle age is patently absurd. You're a very attractive woman. If you were single and unencumbered, I confess I'd be extremely tempted, but, as it is, thanks but no, thanks. Now if you would let go of my clothes, I'd like to get on.'

She looked down, stunned to discover that her hands had wound into the soft cotton of his shirt. The warmth of his hard chest seemed suddenly scorching, and she released him abruptly, stepping back as if to distance herself from such unwarranted intimacy.

His eyes were laughing at her, and as he strode away she could have sworn that she heard a soft chuckle.

Well, damn him. Who needed his friendship anyway? She marched into her office, got the number of the hospital from Andrea the Android and phoned Mr Hart about Sam Carver.

She was just clearing the table after their evening meal when there was a clatter on the stairs and someone pounded on her front door.

'Coming,' she called, and, handing the plates to Delphine to wash, she went to the door.

It was Max, towering over her, looking bigger than ever and obviously hopping mad.

'Can I help you?' she asked with forced politeness.

'Yes,' he gritted, his voice icy with control. 'You can ask your au pair to keep her clothes on in the garden. I've had my handyman bending my ear for the past half-hour, giving me a rundown on the state of youth today, and it's not an experience I'm in a hurry to repeat!'

Cathy blinked. 'I'm sorry, I don't know what you're talking about——'

'Well, then, I suggest you ask her. He couldn't get any work done today because he was unable to get to the workshop. I gather she was lying out here on the grass virtually naked for four hours — apart from the danger to herself of skin cancer, she practically gave Stan a stroke!'

Cathy couldn't help herself. The giggle rose up and bubbled out, and after a second's struggle, Max chuckled.

'I'm sorry,' she managed eventually.

'So am I. Just have a word, could you?'

'Of course. And please apologise to Stan for me.'

'And risk another ear-bashing? No way! How are you settling in, by the way? I've been meaning to come up and see you, but I've been too busy.'

'Oh, we've settled in well. It's a lovely flat. I know John engineered it, but I can't say I'm sorry. We're very happy here.'

'Good. I'm sorry if I seemed unwelcoming, but he's becoming a bit obsessive about me. Wants me married off, I think.'

Cathy grinned wryly. 'I know the feeling. My mother-in-law would like to see me settled with someone else, and she just won't take no for an answer.'

They shared a smile rich with understanding, and Cathy's naturally hospitable nature responded automatically.

'Would you like to come in and have a cup of coffee? I'm afraid I haven't got anything stronger to offer you.'

He shook his head. 'I haven't really got time. I've got some paperwork I really ought to get on with. Thank you anyway.'

'You're welcome — oh, before you go, I just wondered — there's a locked door, presumably leading to the house?'

'Yes, that's right. These rooms used to be the butler's

quarters. The door opens on to the back stairs and comes out on the landing. Why?'

'I just wondered—Stephen can be awfully noisy, and I didn't want to disturb you. I—I mean, I didn't know where you sleep. . .'

He grinned lazily. 'No problem. You won't disturb me, my room's at the other end of the house.'

A sudden image of Max sprawled asleep across a huge four-poster bed leapt unbidden into her mind, and Cathy flushed.

'Oh. Good. That's fine, then.' She struggled with a smile.

'Why did you want to know where I sleep?' he asked, idly tucking an escaped strand of her hair back behind her ear.

'I—I didn't! I wanted to be sure we didn't disturb you.'

He chuckled softly. 'You've been disturbing me since the moment I clapped eyes on you, Catherine. It's very gratifying to know it's mutual.'

She rallied her scattered defences and straightened away from him. 'What are you talking about?' she asked, flustered. 'I'm not the least bit interested in you, Dr Armstrong. You're not at all my type, and, even if you were, I've told you, that part of my life is over, finished with! I have Stephen to think about now, and dallying with you in the sunset doesn't figure very highly in my plans!'

He cast his eyes over his shoulder, and turned back with a smile. 'What sunset?'

The sun was still well above the horizon, and Cathy flushed. 'You know what I mean. Please, Max!'

'My pleasure,' he said softly, and moved closer.

'Well, it wouldn't be mine,' she retorted, desperately trying to put distance between them on the little landing. She bumped against the door-frame, and he closed the gap slightly. 'You're deliberately misunderstanding me! I meant what I said, you aren't my type. I expect you're the sort of macho guy who kisses his women until their lips bleed!'

The corner of his mouth lifted slightly. 'I have it on good authority that I'm a very gentle lover,' he answered, quite undeterred. 'I'd be quite happy to satisfy your curiosity.'

Cathy's breath caught in her throat, her wilful imagination racing.

'I'm not curious!' she denied weakly.

'Liar,' he murmured, his voice gravelly and soft.

She moaned. 'I can't believe we're having this conversation!'

Reaching up, he plucked a rose from above the door and held it against her cheek. 'You've got beautiful skin,' he said huskily. 'Velvety, like the petals of a rose. It's even the same delicate peach.'

Soft colour flooded her cheeks at his words.

'You're talking like a romantic fool,' she said breathlessly, and a slow smile tilted his sensuous lips.

'You blush like a virgin,' he murmured, scanning her cheeks with amused fascination. 'How can a woman who's been married and widowed and is raising a child alone still colour up at a simple compliment? Unless she, too, is a romantic fool?'

'Max, stop it!' she protested feebly.

His eyes clashed with hers, the vivid blue burning with some nameless emotion she didn't dare to define.

'You've got very kissable lips,' he said softly, so

softly that if she hadn't had her eyes fixed firmly on his own very kissable lips she would have missed it.

'Max, no!' she moaned as his head came down.

'Yes,' he murmured against her lips, and then there was nothing but the feel of his mouth against hers, draining her resistance as if it had never been.

With a sigh of surrender she leant into him, feasting on the contrast between her softness and his hard, lean frame. His hands slid down her back and urged her against him, and her body went up in flames, aching for the pleasure so long denied.

With a whimper she wriggled closer, and he made a guttural noise low in his throat as he dragged his mouth away from hers to trail hot, open-mouthed kisses over the warm skin of her throat.

Then he lifted his head, and her hands came up to pull it down again.

His fingers fastened gently over her wrists and eased her hands away.

'Now tell me I'm not your type,' he said softly, and released her, turning on his heel to run lightly back down the stairs, leaving her slumped against the doorframe, speechless.

CHAPTER THREE

CATHY found it impossible to sleep that night. Every time the soft shrouds of oblivion drifted closer, her mind seemed to float free into a world of sensation that she had long dismissed, a world of murmured sighs and tender caresses, of spiralling passion and earth-shaking emotions that left her aching with frustration and loneliness.

She turned on her bedside light and tried to read, but the words failed to hold her attention and she gave up in despair, getting up to tiptoe quietly into the kitchen and make a cup of tea.

The sky was lightening, and, letting herself out silently, she crept down the steps and walked barefoot through the dewy grass. The air was blissfully cool on her overheated skin, and she lifted her face to the sky, absorbing the early morning scents and sounds of the countryside.

Her feet carried her round the side of the house on to the terrace behind it, and she found a short flight of steps leading down on to a broad swath of lawn.

She had never been round the back into the main part of the garden and she found it fascinating to sit on the steps sipping her tea and watching as the dawn lightened the sky and colour slowly seeped into the borders, turning the garden into a brilliant riot of hues all jostling for her attention.

Further down the garden she could see the duck

pond, and beside it the ducks slept, their heads tucked under their wings, their coats glossy with dew, and in the field beyond she could see rabbits, the young ones already frisky even this early in the day.

She laughed softly at their antics, content to sit and watch them a little longer.

After a while she felt a strange prickling in the back of her neck, a sort of awareness, as if she were no longer alone. Turning her head, she studied the back of the house, the stone-mullioned windows marching like sentries across the upper storey. She scanned them, wondering which one, if any, was Max's room. He had said he slept at the far end of the house, but which of the end rooms?

She watched silently for several seconds, but there was no sign of life, however, and none of the curtains was closed; she finally concluded that he must sleep at the front of the house.

Crazy, she thought, returning her eyes to the view over the garden to the hills beyond. Why would he want to look out of the front when from the back he could see the sun rise?

The first brilliant arc appeared as she sat there, edging over the hills to her left and pouring over the landscape like molten gold. She felt peace steal into her heart—peace, and the realisation that she was more vibrantly alive now, this morning, than she had been for years. Like Sleeping Beauty after the Prince had kissed her, she thought.

But unlike Sleeping Beauty, she had responsibilities. She still had Stephen to think of, and he above all must come first.

Rising stiffly from the cold stone of the steps, she

made her way over the damp grass towards the house, pausing briefly to stare again at the end window; then, head bowed, she crossed the terrace and went back round the side of the house, quite unaware of the man who stood watching her from the shadows of his room.

He shouldn't have kissed her. It had been a big mistake—though not the first. The first, perhaps, had been to treat her like Pauline, expecting that she would shirk her responsibilities, failing to follow through as her predecessor had done.

Of course it was still early days, but after his phone call to Sam Carver he had realised his mistake. She had apparently been meticulously thorough in her explanations, soothing his fears without in any way denying the seriousness of his condition.

Max knew he owed her an apology for that—though not the kiss. God, no. That kiss. . .

His body heated at the memory, and he groaned softly as she stood up, her body clearly outlined by the early rays of the sun which turned the fine cotton of her nightgown to gossamer, clinging softly to her lush curves as she flitted through the damp grass like a pixie. The sun danced in her hair, so that it seemed like a halo of red and gold curls that tumbled over her shoulders in soft profusion.

Just before she turned the corner she glanced back, seeming to look straight at him, and her face was etched with determination and—sorrow?

He sighed heavily and turned away from the window. Damned if he could sleep now with the image of her body imprinted on his senses like a dream, caught in the half-world between sleep and wakefulness.

Well, he was awake now—wide awake and aching with frustration. He tugged on his old cut-off shorts and a pair of ancient trainers, and, whistling softly to the dog, he let himself out of the house. Perhaps a run would take the edge off this blazing need so that he could get through the day without disgracing himself by dragging her on to the carpet and making wild, passionate love to her in front of everyone!

The day was easier to deal with than the night had been. The computer decided to be friendly, the patients were welcoming, and Max was blissfully absent, taking a surgery in one of the outlying villages. The only fly in the ointment was Andrea, who persisted in her chilly way to contrive to make Cathy feel unwelcome.

She ignored her, talking instead to the practice nurse, Sarah, and John Glover, who, having decided he had been hasty throwing Max and Cathy together, was doing his best to atone by mothering her to bits.

She took an antenatal clinic that afternoon, and was just about to start her evening surgery when Max tapped on the door and walked in.

'Have you got time for a quick word?' he asked.

She glanced at her watch pointedly. 'Very quick.'

He grinned ruefully. 'I won't hold you up. I owe you an apology for yesterday. I didn't behave very well, and I was obviously rather unfair to you. I'm sorry.'

She was amazed. The great Max Armstrong, lover of the decade, apologising for gracing her with his attention? Remarkable!

'Forget it,' she dismissed. 'It was just a simple kiss——'

'Kiss?' He laughed softly. 'Oh, you misunderstand,

Catherine. I wasn't apologising for kissing you, and I don't intend to. I was talking about Sam Carver. I implied that you might not have been able to reassure him. It was wrong of me.'

'Well, well. What made you see the light?' she asked with a trace of sarcasm to cover her confusion.

'I spoke to him last night, and he phoned me a little while ago and told me he's seen David Hart this morning. Apparently he knew exactly what to expect, because you'd filled in all the gaps and left nothing out.'

'I did try. So how did he get on?'

'You were right, they think it's CA testis. He goes in tomorrow for his orchidectomy, and apparently Hart is confident it's in the very early stages. They'll use radio-opaque tumour markers to see if the level falls significantly after the operation. If it does, of course, that means that the tumour was likely to have been restricted to the testicle. If not. . .' He shrugged. 'He'll be referred to the oncologist next week for a CAT scan and they'll decide the treatment based on that and the histology of the lump.'

'Oh, dear,' she sighed. 'It's nice to be right, but I wish I'd been wrong. How did he sound?'

'Calm, resigned. He's told his wife, and she's taken it very well. One bit of good news—seems she's just found out she's pregnant anyway, so she'll be in to see you fairly soon, I expect.'

'Mmm.'

'Mmm?'

She shrugged. 'Let's just hope he makes it. Pregnancy and a death sentence make pretty odd bedfellows.'

He perched on the corner of her desk.

'You were pregnant when you found out about your husband, weren't you?'

She nodded. 'We got the results the same week. Of course, we never dreamt then that Michael would die in two years. Most cases of MS are much slower, but his was particularly rapid. He had no remission at all, just a relentless decline.'

'It must have been hell.'

'I suppose so. I can hardly remember it. I was working, and Joan was looking after Michael and Stephen for me, and in the end he went into a hospice.' She lifted one shoulder expressively. 'It all seems very long ago.'

'Three years?'

'Nearly four. He died in August.'

'That's a long time to lock yourself away.'

She met his curiously intense gaze briefly, and dropped her eyes.

'Have dinner with me tonight.'

The invitation caught her by surprise, and she fumbled for an excuse.

'I—I can't. Delphine has the evening off.'

'We can eat at home, after you get Stephen to bed. We'll leave the communicating door open so you can hear him.'

She floundered, her naturally gregarious soul longing for adult company, but the ingrained habit of years of self-denial rising up to swamp her.

'I won't take no for an answer. You have to eat—I'll make it something simple. Salad or something.'

Still she hesitated.

'It's easy. You open your mouth and you say,

"Thank you, Max, that would be lovely". On the count of three. One, two——'

She looked up into his laughing eyes. 'Thank you, Max, that would be lovely,' she said in a rush.

He slid his thigh off the corner of her desk and straightened, throwing her a lazy smile.

'Good girl. I'll see you at eight. Oh, and by the way——' he paused at the door '——that was not just a simple kiss, and you know it.'

Hot colour flooded her cheeks as he left the room, and it had barely receded before the first patient came in.

'I'm sorry to keep you waiting; we had an emergency case conference,' she said briskly, and told herself that it was almost true. They *had* discussed Sam Carver. She dredged up a smile. 'Now, what's the problem?'

At two minutes to eight she let herself out of her flat, ran down the steps and made herself walk calmly up to Max's heavy oak front door. For some unaccountable reason her pulse was racing and her skin felt flushed. She had scraped her hair back into a bun to make herself look businesslike, but there was nothing she could do about the soft glow to her skin or the light that danced in her eyes. She was going out, at a man's invitation, for the first time since Michael had started dating her nine years before, and the long-forgotten excitement had turned her into an adolescent again, seething with fearful anticipation.

Which was ridiculous, because, for all his fine words, when it came down to it what would Max want with a widow of thirty-five who had lost her figure and was well on the downhill slide to middle age?

Suddenly depressed, she almost turned tail and ran, but as she hesitated Max waved to her from a window.

'Door's open,' he called. 'Come on in.'

It was standing slightly ajar, and she pushed gently and stepped inside.

She was immediately engulfed in a mass of flying fur and slurping pink tongue.

'Penny!' Max roared, and the fur and tongue subsided to the floor in a wriggling heap of eager black and white spaniel.

Laughing, Cathy straightened her dress and looked up into his apologetic eyes.

'Sorry about that, she's a little enthusiastic!' he said gruffly. 'Come on in. Penny, in your bed!'

He led her through to the kitchen, a huge room on the right of the hall and next to the stables. Penny trotted at his heels, a slave to her master, and curled in her bed, watching him under twitching black brows as he went about his preparations.

'Nearly done. What can I get you to drink? G and T, or white wine?'

'Oh, I —'

'Come on, you're not driving!'

She smiled. 'Gin and tonic would be lovely, thank you.'

He poured two generous splashes of gin into tall tumblers, half filled them with ice and lemon and topped them up with tonic.

'Cheers!'

She touched her glass against his, and met his eyes, surprised by the sudden flare of awareness that rippled through her.

She looked away. 'What about the communicating

door? We ought to open it in case Stephen needs me,' she said, clearly reminding him where her priorities lay.

'I'll do it now.'

He opened a door on the other side of the kitchen and ran up the back stairs. While he was gone she looked around. The ceiling was heavily beamed, the units hand-built in limed oak blending old and new perfectly. All the appliances were concealed behind matching panels, and the white-tiled floor and work-tops reflected light into what could otherwise have been a dark room.

All it needed was some bunches of herbs and dried flowers hanging from the ceiling, and copper pans on the wall, and it would be straight out of *Homes and Gardens*.

What it lacked, in fact, was a woman's touch, and Cathy felt a sudden shiver of apprehension. What was she doing sitting here, in this very eligible bachelor's lair, allowing her mind to run amok with cosy little domestic details?

'Catherine Harris, you're losing it!' she muttered to herself.

'Losing what?'

She jumped.

'My mind—and do you have to creep up on me?' she said crossly.

He chuckled. 'He's fast alseep. Come on, let's go in the garden.'

The hall ran through the centre of the house from front to back, and he led her through the garden door on to the terrace and down the steps where she had sat that morning, to a little gazebo that was smothered in sweetly scented honeysuckle.

'What about Stephen?' she fretted.

'He's fine, he was out for the count. Relax, Catherine. I'm not about to pounce on you. Contrary to what you seem to think, I'm not a sex-crazed adolescent.'

'I never said that!'

He laughed ruefully. 'You didn't need to, it's written all over you.'

She sighed. He was probably right. The turmoil her mind was in, it would be a miracle if it didn't show. She fiddled nervously with a fold of her skirt, pleating it between her fingers. 'What do you want with me, Max?'

'Tonight? Congenial company, someone to share a meal with.'

She glanced up at him and looked quickly away, perturbed by the curious intensity of his gaze so at odds with his simple words.

'I don't want to be very late, I didn't sleep too well,' she said, already planning her escape.

'I know — I saw you.'

Her head whipped back round to face him. 'What?'

'This morning, on the steps, with the sun pouring over you and your hair like a halo around your head. You looked like a pixie, flitting through the wet grass in your bare feet.'

She swallowed. 'I didn't see you.'

'I stood in the shadows.'

She looked away again, her fingers twisting in the fabric. 'I thought you must sleep at the front. The curtains —— '

'I never shut the curtains.'

'Oh,' she said lamely.

His hand came out and plucked the pins from her hair, his fingers warm and steady against the nape of her neck.

'What are you doing?' she asked breathlessly.

'Letting your hair down — there. That's better. I've been longing to do that since I met you.'

His fingers sifted through the thick mass, teasing it out, spreading it over her shoulders.

Their eyes meshed and held, desire shimmering between them, and then he dragged his gaze away and stood up.

'We ought to go and eat,' he said huskily.

'Yes. . .'

'Inside or out?'

'What?'

'Where do you want to eat?'

She felt as if food would choke her. Perhaps the fresh air would help. Certainly it would be better than being trapped inside with him, alone in an intimacy that would almost certainly drive them beyond the brink of discretion.

'Outside,' she said unsteadily.

'Fine. We'll sit on the terrace. I'll bring everything out.'

'I'll check on Stephen.'

They both knew there was no need, but Max let her go with an understanding smile that somehow made it worse.

By the time she came back down he had taken all the food out to the terrace, and she had pinned up her hair again.

He noticed, but said nothing, as if he realised she would take flight at the slightest pressure.

Instead he seated her courteously, made sure she had all she needed and then entertained her with funny anecdotes and wickedly accurate parodies of some of their patients whom she had met.

Little by little the tightly coiled spring inside her eased and she started to enjoy herself, relaxing in the effortless camaraderie with which he surrounded her.

He brought coffee out on to the terrace and they carried it round the garden, strolling side by side as he told her a little about some of the plants.

He was very knowledgeable but he didn't make her feel ignorant; instead he shared his enthusiasm and took her on a magical tour of times gone by, telling her a brief history of some of the old roses.

As the last rays of the sun slipped over the horizon, he paused by one rose to pluck a bloom and tuck it behind her ear.

'Beautiful,' he said softly. 'This is probably one of the oldest known roses. Just think, for hundreds of years lovers have been picking this rose on warm summer nights to give to each other.'

She could see his eyes in the swiftly fading light, and they seemed to take on all the fire of the sunset, burning with a fierce intensity that made her tremble.

'Max, why me?' she asked him desperately, her voice uneven. 'What could you possibly see in me? I'm years older than you——'

'Only one, and, anyway, age is meaningless. It's how you feel inside——'

'Exactly! Sometimes I feel centuries old inside, and then you come along and open all these doors that I thought were closed forever, and stir everything up again, but I don't know why! What have I got that you want?' she cried softly. 'Leave me alone, Max. Don't play with me. It isn't fair!'

'Shh.' He pulled her gently into his arms and rocked her against his chest, his hands warm and firm against her back. 'I want nothing from you that you aren't prepared to give me.'

She thought of her body, a long way now from the firm, smooth body of the young woman with whom Michael had fallen in love. Would Max want her still if he could see it, the tone lost, the weight that never seemed to go? Of course not.

'You wouldn't want me if you could see me,' she whispered against his shoulder.

'Don't be absurd,' he said harshly, almost angrily. 'You've got no idea how lovely you are, have you? You've got a way of moving, a grace and beauty that could drive a man wild, but you're quite unaware. You make an art-form out of self-denial, to the extent that you can't imagine why anyone else could want you either! Why do you hate yourself so much?'

'I don't hate myself!' she said jerkily.

'Then why won't you allow yourself any pleasure? Why do you constantly punish yourself? OK, Catherine, Michael died, and it was tragic, but gone are the days when the wife was buried alive with her husband! You have a right to happiness——'

'And you think that's what you're offering me?' she cried, stung at his accurate but desperately painful assessment. 'You think a roll in the hay with you will bring me alive again and make me happy? God, the conceit!'

She tried to pull away from him but his fingers coiled round her wrist, jerking her back up against his body so that she felt the shock of the contact right down to her toes. Then his head came down, his mouth hot and hungry, demanding her response.

Fire licked along her veins, swamping her with desire, sweeping away her resistance. She whimpered against his lips and he deepened the kiss, dragging her hard against him so that she could feel his response. The last shreds of her reluctance fell away and she leant into his body, desperate to remove even the slight barriers that still remained. Then, quite suddenly and without any warning, he lifted his head.

'Just remember,' he said, very softly, his voice thrumming with desire, 'you want me, too.'

Shock rolled over her in waves, bringing nausea in its wake. What was she doing? She twisted away from him and this time he let her go, watching her as she ran across the lawn towards the house, desperate to get away from him.

She fell in her mad scramble up the back stairs, scraping her shin, and it was just the last straw. Defeated, she crumpled on the steps, harsh, racking sobs tearing out of her chest.

Gentle hands lifted her, rocking her against a warm, solid chest as he sat holding her in the safety of his arms, and gradually the tears subsided.

'I'm sorry,' she whispered.

'No, I'm sorry. I pushed you too hard. Forgive me.'

She sagged against him, her fight gone.

'You were right.'

'Not to say all that. Not to treat you as I did. You've scraped your leg,' he added.

She lifted her head and glanced down uninterestedly at her shin. 'Mmm.'

'I'll put some antiseptic on it.'

He lifted her easily in his arms and put her down again on the sofa in the corner of the kitchen, while Penny watched them anxiously from her bed.

Max came back, a bowl and cotton wool and antiseptic in his hands, and, lifting her leg so that it lay across his thighs, he bathed the scrape gently, smoothing cream into the graze with gentle fingers.

'I'm sorry to be a nuisance,' she said quietly.

He looked up at her, his eyes reproachful. 'Catherine, stop it. You're putting yourself down again.'

'I don't want just an affair,' she went on bleakly. 'I've had all I can take of heartache. I just want to be left alone to live my life.'

He reached out a hand and brushed his fingers over her still-damp cheek. 'I didn't mean to hurt you.'

'But you would, if you made love to me. I'd be too vulnerable, Max, and I can't allow that to happen.'

'You'd better go, then, while I'm still willing to let you,' he said huskily, 'because the longer you sit there, looking at me with those tear-drenched eyes, the less control I'm going to have over my actions.'

So saying he stood up and pulled her gently to her feet.

'How's the leg?'

'It'll be fine. I'm sorry I turned into a watering-can.'

He smiled, a tender, heart-warming smile that nearly started her off again. 'At a guess I'd say it's a luxury you haven't allowed yourself nearly often enough. Now off you go, and for God's sake lock the door behind you.'

She rose up on tiptoe and brushed her lips against his cheek. 'Thanks for supper.'

'You're welcome.'

He stepped back, ramming his hands into his pockets as if to keep them under control, and, drawing a deep breath, she ran quickly up the stairs, ignoring the pain in her leg, and didn't let out her breath until the door was closed and locked behind her.

The next day was a busy one. Contrary to her expectation she had slept like a log, waking refreshed and ready to take on the world.

When she arrived at the surgery Max greeted her with a smile, and she found it easy to smile back at him, despite the somewhat fraught nature of their parting.

She went into her surgery and to her surprise he followed her.

'How's the leg?'

'All right — a little stiff, but otherwise fine, thanks.'

He nodded. 'Are you OK for duty tonight?'

'Yes, Delphine's all geared to cover me. Why?'

He shrugged. 'Just wondered. I'll see you later.'

He closed the door, and left her wondering just where the harsh, judgemental Dr Armstrong had gone to — or perhaps he had only existed in her imagination?

One of her patients, a Mrs Bickers, seemed at first to be simply there to check her out. She had noticed an element of this in several of the patients and was ready to go along with it, dishing out reassurance and sending them on their way satisfied that the new doctor was all right.

But something about Mrs Bickers troubled her. She complained of a sore throat, but Cathy could see no evidence of any inflamation.

'Perhaps you've strained it, it's easily done.'

'Perhaps.' She paused, as if she was not sure how to continue.

Cathy frowned. There was something wrong, something much bigger than her sore throat.

'Mrs Bickers, do you want to talk about it?' she asked gently.

The woman's face crumpled and she pressed her hand to her mouth, holding back the tears.

'Oh, dear,' Cathy said gently, and took her other hand, offering wordless comfort. After a few moments the woman took a shuddering breath and lifted her head, her pride evident.

'I'm sorry, I — there are things at home. . .'

'Tell me.'

She sniffed. 'Have you got time?'

Cathy glanced down at the pile of notes on her desk.

'Can you hang on twenty minutes? I've got three more people to see, then we can have a long chat. I can find you somewhere to sit and get you a cup of coffee — will you do that?'

The woman nodded, much to Cathy's relief. She didn't want her running away in this fragile state — although there might be little she could do to help Mrs Bickers, she realised, a willing ear would go a long way at the moment.

She found the practice manager in the office.

'I've put Mrs Bickers in the treatment-room — she's

a bit upset and I've said I'll talk to her after I've finished my surgery. I wonder if you could give her a cup of coffee, Andrea?'

Andrea gave her a chilling look. 'You've got calls to make after surgery—and I am rather busy at the moment.'

'So am I—and I'm trying to get on. She has white, no sugar. Thank you.'

'I don't think you quite understand,' Andrea replied coldly. 'I don't have time—it isn't part of my job to run around after patients with cups of coffee, any more than it's yours—and on the subject of job description, what she probably needs at the moment is a priest or a social worker, not a medical practitioner!'

Cathy was furious. 'Don't you dare presume to tell me the limits and parameters of my job! You haven't spoken to her, you have no idea what's troubling her or what treatment she might require—and until I get a chance to talk to her, neither do I! Now kindly do as you've been asked and take her a cup of coffee so that I can get on with my surgery!'

She stormed out of the office, straight into Max.

'Excuse me,' she muttered crossly, pushing past him, and went back to her surgery, still shaking with anger. How dared she?

The last three patients were fortunately dealt with quickly, and she went back into the treatment-room to find an empty coffee-cup sitting there, but no patient.

She went into the office. 'Where's Mrs Bickers?'

Andrea glanced up from the computer. 'She left—said she didn't have time to wait. Max wants to see you, by the way. He's in his room.'

As she turned away, Cathy caught a glimpse of what

could have been a smirk, and her mouth tightened. And to think she had been worried about working with *Max*!

She rapped on his door and he barked a response. Her eyebrow twitched, but she said nothing, merely opening the door and going in.

'Andrea said you wanted to see me.'

'Yes — about Mrs Bickers — or anybody else, come to that. Never, ever, put anyone in the treatment-room alone. There are syringes, needles, all manner of things which could be stolen and misused. If you need more time to see someone, either ask them to make another longer appointment, or put them back in Reception to wait until you have time —'

'But she was crying! She was obviously worried and depressed about something, and she needed privacy and help.'

'Not that badly, evidently, or she would have stayed. Quite apart from which, we're a medical practice, not a drop-in centre for bored housewives!'

'Max, that's a gross distortion of the facts! In my opinion there was something badly wrong that she needed to talk about —'

'Of course there's something badly wrong! Her husband's a gambler! He's ill — him, not her.'

'Oh, God, why didn't somebody tell me?' she groaned.

'I didn't know you were seeing her — and anyway, it's probably irrelevant.'

'No, I don't think so. It's making her ill — damn it, Max, I saw her —'

'So did I, and she looked fine to me. Catherine,

you've got to toughen up a bit. Life's hard. People cope. You haven't got time to pander to them.'

She was stunned—stunned and horrified. 'Toughen up? How dare you? How dare you sit there in your suit that cost hundreds of pounds, with your country house a few miles up the road and your flashy new Mercedes sitting outside in the car park, and tell me life's tough! What the hell do you know about poverty, about the desperate worry that debt brings, about the fear that your children will go hungry and your home will be repossessed? He might be the one who was ill initially, but, take my word for it, he's making her ill too, and without help she's going to go under! For God's sake, Max, get off your over-privileged backside and get out there in the real world!'

He glared at her coldly. 'Have you quite finished?'

She gritted her teeth. 'For now.'

'Good. There's just one more thing. I gather you ordered Andrea to take Mrs Bickers a cup of coffee.'

'I asked her——'

'Catherine, I heard you order her! That isn't part of her job.'

'It isn't part of mine, either, but if I'd had time I would have done it. It wouldn't hurt the supercilious bitch to exercise a little compassion occasionally.'

Max's mouth tightened in anger. 'I'll have you know that she's an extremely efficient, very highly qualified professional, and her contribution to this practice is enormous!'

'So it might be, but she's still a cold-hearted, in-human robot. No wonder she gets on so well with the computer—frankly, they have a great deal in common, and I don't find either of them user-friendly!'

Turning on her heel, she stormed out of his office and practically fell over Andrea, standing outside with a sheaf of correspondence in her hand.

'Well!' she said, all injured innocence.

'Oh, go and eat nails!' Cathy muttered, and marched past her, snatching up her bag from her room on the way out to her car.

Then she went back in, found Mrs Bickers's notes and added them to the pile waiting for visits.

She tacked her on to the end of the list, and found her at home, hanging out the washing.

There had been no reply at the front door and so Cathy had gone round the back through the side gate, calling out as she went.

'Oh! Hello, Dr Harris!' Mrs Bickers said quietly, her eyes flicking to the fence as if to check for eavesdroppers. 'I didn't expect to see you here.'

'That's OK. I gather you didn't have time to wait this morning after all, so I thought I'd pop in as I was passing. I hope I'm not here at an inconvenient time.'

'Oh, no—not at all. I was just putting the washing out. Let me put these last two things up and I'll be with you. I can't believe the lovely weather we're getting, all this sunshine. I expect we'll all get skin cancer next!'

She was babbling nervously, and Cathy got the distinct impression her presence wasn't wanted. A quick glance at the clothes showed that the quality left a great deal to be desired, although the house was pleasant enough, a modern detached house on a little estate on the outskirts of the town. The clothes didn't fit with the rest, and Cathy guessed that the debts from her husband's addiction were biting deeper and deeper.

'You'll have to forgive the mess, I wasn't expecting

anyone,' Mrs Bickers said edgily as they went back down the path to the kitchen door.

'Look, Mrs Bickers, I'm here to help, not to judge you. Please stop worrying and talk to me.'

'Come in — the neighbours,' she said breathlessly, and shut the door firmly behind them.

She was right about the mess. The room was in chaos, although it had once been a very nice kitchen, and it was quite obvious that the woman was at the end of her tether.

Cathy sat her down and extracted a long tale of woe, most of which she had already guessed.

Her husband was an accountant for a local firm, and often brought home work in the evenings — work which, unbeknown to her, had been private accounting work for small firms. It seemed that for years he had lied about the level of his income, using that extra money earned in the evenings to squander hundreds of pounds a month on anything on which he could lay a wager.

She had found out about it quite by accident a year before, and he had broken down and promised never to gamble again.

For a time things had been better, but just recently they had started to slide, and she suspected he had started gambling again.

'I just don't know what to do!' she sobbed. 'I don't know how bad it is, but the other day a letter came in the second post. He didn't tell me what it was, but he was very shaken up, and I think it must have been a threat from a loan shark. And we've had letters from the building society, but he takes all the post to work with him and leaves it there, so I never get to see it!'

'Do you ever go out anywhere?'

She shook her head. 'He never wants to, I think because he's terrified people will know and look at him, and I don't like to suggest doing anything that will cost money because frankly we can't cope as it is!'

Cathy sighed. 'Oh, dear, what a mess. Can you still talk to him, or won't he discuss it?'

'He won't discuss it — says he's given up, he promised me he would and he has, but he can't look at me when he says it, and our sex life's come to a grinding halt. Well, how can you make love to someone when you can't trust them any more? He's even been stealing money out of my purse. I have to hide the housekeeping, and even then sometimes he finds it. I cut up my cashpoint card so he couldn't take the money out of my bank account, and he started stealing the children's pocket money! When he's desperate enough he'll find it from somewhere, and there's always his salary.'

'Have you thought of having his salary paid direct to you?'

Her head snapped up and she laughed, a shrill, nervous sound that grated on Cathy's nerves. 'He wouldn't hear of it.'

'He might, at some point, if he was desperate enough. Then once it was done, you could handle all the finances. It's been done before, and it works very well. The same thing often works for manic depressives. If the opportunity arises, think about it — and do come and see me if you're worried about him or yourself.'

She nodded, and chewed her lip hesitantly. 'I'm sorry I got you into trouble. I heard you having a row with that Andrea girl — she lives a few doors away. Nasty piece of work.'

Cathy defended her automatically. 'She's very efficient, and invaluable in the practice.'

Mrs Bickers chuckled, showing the woman she had been before her troubles had destroyed her. 'I dare say. Dr Armstrong brought me the coffee, by the way. She was too busy. Don't know what he sees in her, frankly. I expect that's why she dislikes you, as you're living with him.'

Cathy flushed. 'I'm hardly living with him, Mrs Bickers. I rent his flat, and believe me, I'm well chaperoned. I live there with my son and our au pair.'

Mrs Bickers shot her a keen look. 'Are you divorced?'

'No, widowed.'

'Oh, I'm sorry.'

Cathy gave her a gentle smile. 'So am I. He was a good man.'

'They say the good die young.'

Their eyes met in a moment of understanding. Their situations werc vastly different, but in their own way both of them knew sorrow.

Cathy laid a hand on Mrs Bickers's shoulder. 'I must get back, I've got a clinic. Let me know if there's anything I can do.'

She drove thoughtfully back to the clinic. So Mrs Bickers thought Andrea disliked Cathy because she was living at the Manor—and she didn't know what Max saw in Andrea. Did that mean they were having a relationship? And if so, then where did that leave Cathy?

'On your own—where you want to be,' she told herself firmly, but somehow it didn't quite ring true.

CHAPTER FOUR

THE rest of the day passed in a blur, with a routine antenatal clinic followed by evening surgery and further calls.

She popped home at half-past four and spent a few minutes with Stephen, but he seemed more interested in the children's programmes on television than he was in her, so she returned to the surgery.

She made two calls on the way home at six-thirty, and arrived back at seven to find no sign of either Stephen or Delphine.

She looked around their area of the garden, but found nothing, and then just when she had decided that they had probably gone for a walk Delphine strolled up the drive alone.

'Where's Stephen?' Cathy asked frantically.

'With the doctor—they are playing in the garden. Oh, Cathy, what *fantastique* eyes!'

Just then Cathy was so cross with Max that she could have poked his fantastic eyes right out, but she refrained from saying so, more immediately concerned with the fact that Delphine had abandoned Stephen to Max and gone off when she was supposed to be looking after him.

'Delphine, you should be with him—it isn't fair to expect Dr Amstrong to look after him, and I'd rather you didn't ask him. Where have you been?'

She looked instantly crestfallen. 'I 'ad to post a letter

to *Maman*. Stephen and the doctor, they are very 'appy togezzer, 'e is teaching Stephen the cricket—'e said it was OK. I'm sorry, I didn't think you would mind. . .'

'Oh, Delphine—just don't do it again, OK? I'd rather we kept out of Dr Armstrong's way in future.'

Her pretty face fell even further. 'First I get in trouble with my clothes, now this. I think you are very cross with me, no?'

She looked so unhappy that Cathy relented and gave her a hug. 'No, Delphine, I'm not cross with you at all. You and Stephen are getting on very well, and I'm very pleased. I'll go and find him.'

She left the girl looking slightly mollified, and went round into the back garden to find her son.

At first she couldn't see them, then as she went further on to the terrace a movement at the end of the garden caught her eye, and her heart leapt in her throat.

Stephen was lying on the ground, thrashing in agony, and Max was bending over him talking urgently to him. Whatever could have happened? Had he been hit by the ball?

Fear lent wings to her feet, and she ran like lightning down the garden. As she drew nearer she could see that Max had his hands around Stephen's chest, as if he was holding him still, but why?

'What is it? What's the matter?' she cried, and Max turned round, laughter dying on his face as he registered her panic.

'Hey, it's OK.'

'What's happened to him? Why's he lying on the ground?' she slithered to a halt and dropped down beside them.

Stephen grinned up at her. 'Hi, Mum. Max was tickling me.'

Her shoulders sagged with relief, and she didn't know whether to laugh or cry. 'Oh, God, I thought something had happened to him,' she said raggedly.

Max gave her an odd look and let Stephen go. 'Find the cricket bat,' he instructed. 'We'll show your mother what I've taught you.'

As Stephen ran away, the dog at his heels, Max helped Cathy to her feet and frowned swiftly at her. 'You're shaking like a leaf. Whatever did you think was wrong?'

She lifted her shoulders helplessly. 'I had no idea. I'm sorry, I over-reacted.'

One of his eyebrows shot up. 'Well, that's an understatement. OK, Stephen, are you ready?'

Max loped towards him, his long legs eating up the ground, and then bowled a slow, lazy over-arm straight at the bat.

Stephen whacked it with huge enthusiasm and it arced high into the air, clean over the wall to land in the field, swiftly followed by Penny.

'Six! Good man!' Max yelled, and Stephen raised his bat above his head and cheered.

Then he dropped the bat and scrambled over the stone wall into the field to where Penny was sniffing about in the grass, her plumy tail waving furiously.

'Bit further down,' Max called, and then turned his attention back to Cathy.

'About this morning—I know Andrea can be difficult, but making coffee for patients really isn't her job.'

'If that's meant to be an apology, it was a lousy one,' Cathy said bitterly.

Max's eyebrow arched again. 'It wasn't—I don't consider I have anything to apologise for.'

'Hmph,' she snorted. 'How about questioning my professional judgement, for starters? I knew there was something wrong with Mrs Bickers——'

'I thought you said at your interview that you didn't rely on intuition?'

'Not when there's a better method,' she returned sharply, 'but in this case it was justified. I went to see her after I'd done my calls this afternoon. There was something wrong. Her husband's gambling again, and she thinks he's in the grip of a loan shark.'

'Oh, God. Poor woman.'

Cathy gave him a withering look. 'That's all right— life's tough. She'll cope. Stephen? Come now, please.'

'I have to find the ball!'

'Cathy, I didn't mean to be hard——'

'Then you need English lessons. Your vocabulary is obviously more restricted than you'd realised. Stephen, *now*, please!'

'But Mum——'

'Stephen, do as your mother says. I'll find the ball,' Max said, vaulting easily over the wall and walking up to the boy. 'You'd better go now, old son.'

'Bathtime,' he said with disgust.

Max laughed and tousled the fair, springy hair. 'I expect so. Go on, there's a good boy. We can play another time.'

'Really?' He tipped his eager face up to Max, and Cathy's heart contracted at the hero-worship she saw etched on his little features.

Max nodded. 'Really. I promise.'

'Great!'

Stephen ran back to her then, scrambling over the wall and slipping his hand into Cathy's. 'Did you hear?'

'Yes, I heard. Say "thank you for having me".'

The boy parroted her words, and Max's mouth twisted in a wry grin. 'You're welcome.'

Stephen nearly drove her mad for the next half-hour, talking about Max this and Max that, until she could have pushed him under the bathwater and left him there!

Instead she fished him out of the bath, towelled him roughly dry and pulled on his pyjamas. 'Come and read to me, and tell me what you've done at school,' she said in a desperate attempt to change the subject.

'We had cricket—that's why Max was teaching me. He used to play cricket for the county, and he still plays sometimes for Barton. He's playing on Sunday afternoon—can we go and watch?'

Cathy groaned and gave up. 'I expect so, unless I'm on duty.'

'No, you're not. Max said Dr Glover was on duty this weekend, so you'd be able to bring me. He seemed quite pleased.' Stephen twisted round in her lap and peered up at her searchingly. 'Do you like him?'

She stifled the groan. 'He can be very nice.'

'I think he's great. He really didn't mind playing with me at all—he said so, lots of times. If I had a dad, I'd like him to be like that. Was my dad like that?'

Cathy floundered. Michael had, in fact, been fairly indifferent to Stephen, but whether because of his illness or because he didn't take naturally to fatherhood she would never know.

'I'm sure he would have been if you'd been old enough to play with,' she compromised, and opening his reading book, she read with him until his eyelids drooped. Then she slid him into bed, kissed his cheek and left him, wandering absently out of the front door to sit on the top step, gazing blindly into the distance.

She had often wondered what life would have been like if Michael had lived. Different, certainly, but she had never been sure how much he had wanted children. Perhaps he wouldn't have been a good father? He had been a good husband in the times when things were going well for them, but when he had become ill he had often been difficult to live with.

Except at the end. Shortly before he died he seemed to come to terms with what was happening, and he had devoted what little energy he had to Cathy and Stephen, encouraging her to talk about her feelings and sharing his worries for her future. And after his death, curiously, she had felt his presence very strongly, guiding her through the difficult times, the landmarks and anniversaries that lay like a minefield ahead of her for the first year or two.

Recently, though, he hadn't seemed to be there, almost as if he felt she could cope now. In fact, she could hardly remember him any more. Perhaps that explained her loneliness, the restlessness that plagued her at night, the strange images and unsettling sensations that stalked her dreams.

Delphine brought her her salad, and she sat on the steps picking at it while the scent of the apricot roses drifted all around her on the heavy evening air, bringing with it the memory of the feel of Max's arms around her, the hard strength of his body and the subtle fragrance of his skin.

Dear God, she hardly knew him and yet he seemed

to fill her thoughts almost to the exclusion of common sense. Almost. If she hadn't run away last night, what would have happened? Would they have made love — almost total strangers, driven by this elemental physical force that thrust reason aside and dragged them helplessly in its wake?

The phone rang, bringing her back to reality with a jolt. It was Elaine Bickers.

'I'm sorry to trouble you,' she began tearfully, 'but please come. We've had a dreadful row and he's locked himself in the bedroom, and I'm terrified he'll do something stupid — please help me. . .'

'Don't worry. Just keep calm, go and sit outside the door and try to make him talk to you, and I'll be with you in a minute.'

Delphine appeared behind her. 'You are going out, yes?'

'Yes, I'm afraid so. That is all right, isn't it? You will be here?'

'*Mais oui*, of course. But you 'ave not finished your salad.'

Cathy smiled. 'Save it — I'll be back later.'

She drove swiftly to the Bickerses' house, and the door was flung open almost as she pulled up outside.

Mrs Bickers ran to the car, wrenching the door open and tugging at Cathy's arm. 'Oh, please hurry, I think he's trying to kill himself!'

She ran up the path and through the door, and Cathy followed her up the stairs and caught her arm.

'It might be an idea if you tell me what started it,' she said softly.

Mrs Bickers nodded, and led Cathy into a little bathroom at the back of the house.

'I told him about our conversation—suggested he had his money paid into my account so that I could handle all the bills, but he went wild and accused me of not trusting him, so I asked him about the letters——'

'Is that when he hit you?' Cathy asked gently.

Her hand flew up to her cheek, to cover the livid bruise that flowered over the side of her face.

'I told him our marriage was going to pieces and he said what did I expect, when I wouldn't let him near me, and then he. . . Oh, God.'

'Are you all right?'

She nodded and sniffed hard, dashing away the tears from her cheeks.

'I don't want Tom to kill himself. However I feel about him, whatever else happens, it's not worth dying for.'

'Why don't you go and put the kettle on while I talk to him?' Cathy suggested gently.

Reluctantly, Mrs Bickers agreed, and, showing Cathy which room her husband was in, she went downstairs, glancing repeatedly over her shoulder.

Cathy stood outside the door for a moment listening, and then tapped gently. 'Mr Bickers? It's Dr Harris. Could you open the door so we can have a chat without waking the children?' she said quietly.

Silence. She tapped again. 'Mr Bickers? I know you're in there. Please open the door.'

'Go away!' he mumbled. 'Leave me alone. I don't want to talk to anybody.'

'Mr Bickers, why won't you let me help you? If we could just talk this through, I'm sure there's a great deal that could be done to make things easier for all of you——'

'There's nothing you can do. No one can help me. Just leave me alone to die.'

Cathy closed her eyes. How to deal with this one?

'I can't do that, Mr Bickers, I'm a doctor. My job is to make your life worth living, and I can't do that if you won't talk to me. Please let me in.'

'I'm not worth it,' he said raggedly, 'I'm not worth worrying about.'

'Well, worth it or not,' she persisted, 'I am worried about you, and so is your wife, and I'm sure the children care very much about what happens to you.'

'They're better off without me,' he mumbled. 'What can I give them? We can't afford to take them anywhere, and we never will be able to—if you knew the debts. . .'

His wife returned at that moment, and Cathy put her finger to her lips.

'Why don't you tell me about it?' she suggested.

There was a pause, then the bed creaked as though he was sitting up.

'There's a guy—a loan shark.'

'And you owe him money?'

'Thousands—nearly twenty thousand, I think. I don't know. The interest adds up, it could be more now. He's starting to threaten me—I can't tell Elaine, she doesn't deserve to be worried, but I don't know how to cope any more on my own.'

'You don't have to cope on your own,' Cathy assured him. 'There are plenty of people who can help you if you'll only talk to them.'

'I can't,' he whispered, and Cathy had to strain to

hear him. 'I'm so ashamed. I thought I could lick it on my own, but I can't. It's like a hungry disease, eating away at me, draining everything I've got and more, until there's nothing left to give it. Then you have to lie and cheat and steal—oh, God, help me. I don't want to die, but I can't go on any more!'

He was sobbing now, harsh, broken sobs that were heartrending in the quiet house.

'Tom, open the door,' Cathy said firmly. 'You don't have to face this alone.'

After a few agonising seconds, they heard the lock click and the door swung inwards.

He was a tall man, but his shoulders were bowed with shame and misery, and when he caught sight of his wife's bruised face his own twisted with remorse.

'Oh, God, what have I done to you?' he whispered, and, reaching out his arms, he gathered her to his chest and buried his head in her shoulder.

Cathy went past them into the bedroom. They ignored her, standing holding each other and crying, while she searched the room for any sign of pills that he might have taken.

There was a small bottle of tranquillisers, almost empty, and nothing else immediately obvious.

She laid a hand on his shoulder. 'Tom? Did you take anything? Any pills?'

He nodded his head. 'A few Valium. Not enough. I was going to, but I'm too much of a coward even to do that properly.'

'Perhaps because you realised that it isn't the answer,' she suggested, and he shrugged helplessly.

She gave his shoulder a quick squeeze. 'Come on,

you need to go to hospital. We can talk later when we know you'll be all right.'

She made the arrangements to admit him while his wife packed his case, and while they waited for the ambulance Cathy watched them both.

As the ambulance men helped Mr Bickers into the back of the ambulance, Cathy drew Mrs Bickers to one side.

'Come and see me when he's out, and I'll get you some support organised,' she said. 'I think you could find the psychiatric social worker very helpful.' At Mrs Bickers's agreement, she told her she would make the necessary arrangements in the morning after talking to her husband's consultant.

Then she went home, exhausted, to fall into bed. It was two o'clock, and within an hour the phone had rung again, calling her out to an elderly man with chest pains.

She admitted him and crawled back into bed, only to stagger out again less than two hours later for another call, a child with a sickness bug.

By the time she got home Stephen and Delphine were up and having breakfast, and she joined them wearily, wondering how she was going to get through the day.

'You look shattered.'

Cathy gave a short, humourless laugh. 'Thank you, Max, I feel much better now.'

He grinned and dropped into a chair opposite her in the surgery kitchen. 'Coffee?'

'Thank you.' She shoved her mug across the table to him and sighed heavily.

'Bad night? I heard the car a couple of times.'

'Yes—Tom Bickers tried to top himself.'

His hand stilled in the act of pouring the coffee, and he glanced at her over his shoulder. 'Really?'

'Would I lie to you?' she asked drily.

Max shook his head wonderingly. 'I had no idea it'd got that bad. What did you do?'

She shrugged. 'Talked him out of the bedroom, persuaded him to let me get him into hospital to be pumped out, and then into the psychiatric unit for assessment and therapy—he's dreadfully depressed, and, frankly, so would I be in his position. They're in a hell of a mess.'

'Debts?'

She picked up her coffee. 'You could say that. He's being threatened by a loan shark. He owes him about twenty thousand.'

'Ouch.' Max pursed his lips, then met her eyes ruefully. 'It seems I owe you an apology. I'm sorry if I seemed unsympathetic, I hadn't realised things had reached that point. Do you think she'll stick by him?'

Cathy shrugged again. 'Who knows? They had a fight and he knocked her about last night, before he went and shut himself up in the bedroom.'

Max's eyes widened. 'Is she OK?'

'I think so—hard to tell. I don't think it helped their relationship.'

'I should imagine not.' He drained his coffee and stood up. 'I'll see you later, I've got more patients to see.'

'Me too.'

She went back to her surgery and found that her last patient that morning was Elaine Bickers.

Her eye had almost completely closed up now, and the livid bruise on her cheek was colouring up beautifully. Cathy smiled at her and waved at the chair.

'Come and sit down. How are things?'

She lifted her shoulders expressively. 'Oh, you know — they pumped him out and filled him up with charcoal and put him to bed, and I went in to see him this morning after I took the children to school and he's all very sorry and all that, but — well, it doesn't change anything, does it?'

'That depends on how genuinely sorry he is. I'll ask for a referral to a psychiatrist, and maybe this time we'll have some joy, but until he's ready to stop he won't change. Maybe he's desperate enough now.'

Mrs Bickers shrugged again. 'God knows. If he isn't, I don't know how much more I can take.'

Cathy leant over and looked carefully at her eye.

'That's a real shiner he's given you. Are you OK?'

'I'll live. Actually, I wanted to ask you something. There's a pill — the morning-after pill I think it's called.'

Cathy nodded.

'Does it work?'

'If you take it within three days and you aren't already pregnant at the time of intercourse, then yes, it usually works very well.'

'Oh. Right.'

'Why?' Cathy prompted gently.

'Oh, it's just — last night — well, I said our marriage was going to pieces and he said it already had, and then — I tried to stop him, but he wouldn't listen. . .' She shrugged helplessly. 'I — just couldn't cope with the thought of being pregnant now, not with all this to deal with. It's bad enough without adding to it, and I thought — well, if I could stop a baby starting. . . I couldn't have an abortion, but I wasn't sure how this worked.'

'By suppressing implantation if fertilisation has occurred, but you know, if this is likely to happen again you perhaps ought to consider some more permanent form of contraception, like the Pill or an IUCD.'

'A coil?'

'Yes. It's always there, you don't have to think about it so there's no possibility of unprotected intercourse — it might be worth thinking about for the future.'

'What future? I'm not sure we have one.'

Cathy's heart went out to her. What kind of life was it, trapped by loyalty and the sanctity of marriage vows to a man who was hurtling down the path of self-destruction, and dragging his family after him? And she was trapped, without a doubt, because if she left him and he killed himself how would she live with herself? So there they were, locked into a stalemate with nothing to look forward to unless someone could convince him to put the brakes on his destructive urges before it was too late for them all.

She wrote out the prescription for a course of PC4 pills, told Mrs Bickers to take two as soon as possible, two twelve hours later and come back when she had her next period for the fitting of her IUCD.

'These pills might make you feel a bit sick,' she warned, 'and if your period is late we ought to run a pregnancy test just to be on the safe side, but you should be all right.'

She ushered the woman to the door and watched her go, obviously considerably relieved to have at least that one extra burden removed from her fragile shoulders, and then went home and crawled into bed.

She was woken by Stephen coming in from school full of beans, and managed a sleepy hello before he rushed out of the door again, mumbling something about Max.

'Max, Max, Max,' she grumbled, rolling over into the pillow and sighing. She ought to stop him persecuting the man, but, if he didn't mind, Stephen seemed to be gaining enormously from contact with him.

Deciding he was big enough and ugly enough to fend off a five-year-old if he really wanted to, she slid back into sleep, waking an hour later feeling much more refreshed.

She showered quickly, and, dressing in a pretty print skirt and matching blouse, she went out into the garden to find them.

There was no trace of them in the garden, and she went round to the front to ring the bell.

As she passed the kitchen window, Max tapped on it and beckoned.

'Come on in, the door's open,' he called, and she pushed the heavy door and made her way into the kitchen.

Stephen was sitting up at the kitchen table with a big glass full of a cloudy liquid, and a huge slab of dark, sticky gingerbread.

'Hi, Mum!' he chirruped.

'Hi yourself. Are you quite sure you've got enough?'

Max grinned. 'Leave the kid alone, he's growing. Fancy a glass of lemonade? Agnes made it this afternoon, and it's fantastic.'

She hesitated. He was standing there, just feet away

from her, dressed only in the skimpiest pair of cut-off shorts she had ever seen, displaying acres of smooth, tanned skin with a faint sheen of sweat, and soft golden curls arrowing down across his board-flat stomach and disappearing enticingly under the gaping top button of the shorts. They rode low on his narrow hips, and his long, bare legs were firm and straight, scattered with more of the same soft curls. There were little tufts of hair on his toes, she noticed distractedly, and then flushed, because he had taken the cool glass of lemonade in his hand and rolled it across the board-like contours of his stomach.

'Bliss,' he sighed, and then held the glass out to her. 'Try it.'

She reached out her hand for the glass, taking it automatically and sipping the icy liquid, unable to think of anything except the way he had rolled the glass over his skin. Lifting her chin, she pressed the glass to her throat and sighed softly.

'Good, isn't it?' he said.

'Wonderful,' she murmured, and then met his eyes. 'It's very hot today.'

'You look as cool as a mountain stream,' he said, and his voice was gravelly and deep, husky with desire. His fingers reached out and curled around the glass, brushing against her throat, and he lifted the glass to his lips and drained it, his eyes still locked with hers.

'Mummy, I told Max we'd go to watch him play cricket on Sunday,' Stephen said suddenly, shattering the tension.

'Oh. Right,' she agreed, somewhat absently, and then fussed about with his crumbs to dispel the awkward silence that followed.

'Ricky's going to be there, too — his dad plays for the team as well. He says we'll get a t'riffic tea afterwards.'

'All you ever think about is your stomach,' she grumbled affectionately, and Max laughed.

'Good, healthy appetite, son, isn't it?' He ruffled the boy's hair gently, and Cathy looked away, suddenly shaken by the open affection between the two of them. Was it wise to let Stephen get so close to him? Perhaps she ought to have a word, warn Max how easily children could make attachments so that Stephen wouldn't be hurt when Max got bored with his role of philanthropist.

Because he would get bored, and Cathy didn't know how Stephen would cope when his idol tumbled to the dust.

CHAPTER FIVE

SUNDAY was another scorcher, the July sun beating down on the pitch and driving the supporters into the shade of the great oaks that lined the field.

Here the grass was longer, and the air was filled with the scent of blossom and the heavy drone of bees, the sharp thwack of leather on willow and the muted cheers of the crowd. Every now and then there was a ragged splatter of applause when one of the batsmen scored, and Cathy lay back among the sweet-smelling clover and let it all wash over her.

Every few minutes she lifted her head and scanned the crowd for Stephen and his friend Ricky, and sometimes he would run up to her to tell her what new game they were playing, or to keep her in touch with the score.

As she found the scoring quite incomprehensible, she simply smiled, said something innocuous like, 'Oh, jolly good,' and then he would run off again, little legs going like pistons, in search of some other mythical monster to vanquish.

All in all it was very peaceful, until Max came in to bat. Then, quite inexplicably, her senses leapt to attention and she found herself riveted to the taut ripple of the crisp white shirt over his broad shoulders, the sudden explosion of energy when he hit the ball and sprinted up the wicket, the reach of his long legs, and the delight on his face when he scored a six.

She found herself cheering with the home crowd, kneeling up in the grass and clapping wildly, and when he was out, apparently for forty-two, she watched with bated breath as he ran over to join her, flopping down in the cool shade with a grin and a sigh of relief.

'Good grief, it's hot out there. I could murder a cold beer.'

She smiled. 'Will apple juice do? I've got a carton here, I think it's still cool.'

'Oh, lifesaver!'

He reached out a hand and took the little carton from her, and as their fingers brushed a current of desire rippled through her.

She looked quickly away, suddenly aware of the faint scent of healthy sweat coming from his body.

'I should think you could do with a shower,' she said without thinking, and he chuckled.

'Sorry, do I smell atrocious?'.

She flushed. 'Oh, lord,' she groaned, 'I didn't mean it like that. I was just putting myself in your shoes, and I'd be longing for a cold shower.'

'Another one?'

Their eyes clashed, and as she looked away in confusion he reached out a hand and picked the grass off her hair.

'You've been lying down,' he murmured.

She smiled tentatively. 'Well, I tried to follow it but I don't really understand the game. I had enough trouble with hockey.'

'Lethal game. Cricket's much more civilised.' He fell back against the cool grass and sighed. 'Ecstasy,' he murmured. 'Lie down. The captain'll declare in a minute and we can go and have cucumber sandwiches and you can chat to the vicar's wife.'

'Oh, no, do I have to?' She sighed theatrically, and he laughed.

'Not if you don't want do. The Carvers are here, by the way. Sam's out of hospital and looking really very good.'

'Sore, I expect. How did the op go?'

'OK.' He rolled towards her and propped his head on his hand. 'So, what did you think of my score?'

She tilted her head round. 'Now,' she said teasingly, 'do I disappoint you and say I didn't notice, or swell your already massive head by telling you you were wonderful, or shatter your ego by telling you I've seen better?'

He chuckled. 'Forget I asked. Massive head, indeed.' He was watching her lips, and she had an almost overwhelming urge to lick them. As if he knew, his own tongue flicked out and moistened his lips provocatively, and then he rolled on to his front, bringing his body up against hers. Plucking a long blade of grass, he trailed it tantalisingly over her throat, then down to the soft hollow between her breasts.

'Stop it,' she breathed raggedly. 'People will see.'

'What's to see?'

'You—lying almost on top of me, watching me like a cat with a mouse.'

His eyes flicked over her chest, pausing on the soft swell of her breasts above the low neckline of the sundress.

'You look so soft,' he murmured, 'soft and feminine and yielding. You're enough to drive a man insane.'

'Max, stop it!' she pleaded.

'I want you,' he continued, his voice husky with desire. 'You're driving me crazy. I can't sleep, I can't concentrate on anything except the sound of your voice and the way you move — God, Catherine, you could drive me to drink.'

She struggled into a sitting position, scanning the field. 'I need to find Stephen.'

'Stop hiding behind your son,' Max said quietly, his voice serious now. 'There's something between us and it's time you faced it, Catherine.'

She looked back over her shoulder, studying him thoughtfully for a moment. 'I have faced it, Max — faced it and dismissed it. There's no room in my life for you, or any other man. My life belongs to Stephen now.'

'What about you?'

She sighed in exasperation. 'What about me? I'm quite happy with the status quo.'

He raised a brow slightly. 'Are you? Is that why you can't sleep at night? Why I hear you moving around in the kitchen at three in the morning, making drinks to send you off to oblivion? Take it from me, it doesn't work.'

She was saved from the effort of finding a reply by the ragged applause that broke out amongst the spectators.

'They seem to have finished,' she told him, and struggled to her feet, brushing the grass off her skirt and bending to pick up all her bits and pieces.

She glanced up to find his eyes fixed on her cleavage, and straightened, a swift flush of colour running over her skin. Avoiding his eyes, she gathered the rest of her things and set off determinedly towards the little pavilion.

Stephen ran up to her, full of the score and how Barton would surely win, all thanks to Max and his amazing number of runs, and wasn't he fantastic, and would it be all right if he had tea just over there with his friend Ricky and his family?

'Wouldn't you rather have tea with me?' she asked hopefully, desperate for his presence as a shield between herself and Max, but after a long pause for thought Stephen decided that Ricky had the edge over his hero, and abandoned her to her fate.

She was desperately conscious of Max behind her, following determinedly in her footsteps, and she made a quick detour to the Ladies'.

Useless. He was leaning on a tree waiting for her, and as she came out he shouldered himself away from the broad trunk and strolled towards her.

'We're having tea with the Carvers,' he announced, and, with a knowing grin, he wheeled her round and led her over to a small group under one of the trees, totally ignoring her protests about professional distance and Sam not wanting her there, especially considering the nature of his operation.

'Rubbish,' he dismissed, and then it was too late to escape and she was being introduced to Megan Carver, Sam's pretty little Welsh wife, and the Frys, a young couple with a wriggling baby who were engaged in changing a nappy, evidently against the baby's wishes.

Sam apologised for not getting up, and explained with a diffident grin that he was still finding moving a little uncomfortable.

'Well, I'm mortally offended,' Cathy said with a

laugh, and sat on the colourful rug, as far away from Max as she could decently engineer without being conspicuous.

This put her on the edge of the rug next to Megan Carver, and Cathy turned to her with relief.

'I gather congratulations are in order,' she said quietly under cover of the baby's protests.

'Yes—actually, I've been meaning to come and see you, but last week sort of ran away with me, what with Sam having to go to hospital and so on.'

Cathy smiled. 'I can imagine,' she said wryly. 'Anyway, there's no real urgency unless you think everything isn't well.'

Megan wrinkled her nose delicately. 'To be truthful I haven't had time to think about it,' she confessed. 'Since he came to see you last week, all my time and energy have been devoted to Sam.'

Cathy followed Megan's eyes as they tracked to her husband, and they smiled together as he threw back his head and laughed at something Max said.

'He looks well enough. How's he taking it?' Cathy asked.

'Oh—OK. He was fairly quiet on Tuesday after he'd seen Mr Hart, but when I told him I was pregnant he was over the moon. He cried, actually—I probably shouldn't have told you that, he'd hate it if you knew, but there was so much emotion packed into last week, and now I feel like a wrung-out rag!'

Cathy smiled in sympathy. 'Once he's had the CAT scan and the oncologist has seen him you'll have a much clearer idea of what's going on, but you know he caught it very early.'

Megan nodded slowly. 'I know, but. . .'

Cathy reached out and touched her hand in comfort. 'Come and see me when you've got time. You need the antenatal check, and it'll give you a reason to come. You can get everything off your chest in private, then.'

Megan flashed her a grateful smile. 'Thanks, I will.'

They watched Max and Sam for a moment, and then the baby, her nappy secured at last, crawled over to Max and climbed up on to his lap, grabbing fistfuls of shirt to help her.

Max steadied the little girl as she wobbled to her feet on his legs, and then bounced her gently up and down, making her giggle.

Cathy's heart gave a funny little flutter at the tender scene, and she squashed it ruthlessly. So he was good with children. So what?

'It would be nice to see Max married; he'd be a good father,' Megan said thoughtfully, with a pointed glance at Cathy.

Oh, lord, Cathy thought, not another one! I wonder what's next?

'I gather you're living in his flat—it's lovely out there, isn't it? What do you think of the house?'

'Beautiful—what I've seen of it. I've only been in the kitchen and the hall.' And that should stop that rumour, she thought.

Megan eyed her speculatively. 'He's stinking rich, you know.'

Cathy grinned. 'So everyone keeps telling me, and I keep wondering why. Does he have some fatal flaw that only his money can compensate for?'

Megan laughed and apologised. 'I didn't mean to push him at you, but he is rather gorgeous, don't you think? And he needs someone warm and tender to satisfy that romantic streak—not that nasty piece of work he's been taking out recently—you know, that receptionist creature. What's her name? Anthea?'

Cathy watched the baby crawl back to her mother and tug at her blouse. 'Andrea.'

'That's right—yuck. He took her to the squash club ball a few weeks ago, and I hated her on sight. She's like a damn computer—she'd program all the life out of him, and it would be such a shame. No, you're much better.'

Cathy gave a rather strained smile. 'I'm sorry, I'm not going to be able to help. I'm afraid I'm not in the market for a relationship.'

Megan shot Cathy a startled glance. 'Oh—sorry, I rather thought——?'

Just then Stephen arrived, arms out at his sides and making aeroplane noises, and dived head-first on to the rug next to Max.

'Hello, sport,' Max said calmly, and, righting him with one arm, he clamped him against his side and tickled him until he begged for mercy.

'My son,' Cathy said in explanation.

'Oh, God, I didn't realise you were married—I'm sorry. Oh, whatever did you think——?'

'It's all right. I'm a widow, but the same thing still applies.'

Megan closed her eyes in embarrassment. 'Oh, lord, and I've been rambling on—I'm so sorry.'

Cathy forced a smile. 'Look, it's OK. You haven't offended me.'

'Truly?'

'Truly. Please don't apologise.'

Megan shook her head and gave a rueful smile. 'It's

Max's fault — it's the way he's been talking about you, as if — well. . .'

I'll kill him, she thought with unaccustomed violence, and glared at him.

'Oh, dear, have I dumped him in it?'

She laughed. 'No, I would say he's managed it all by himself.'

Megan chuckled. 'Don't be mad. Actually he's very lonely, and he did seem keen.' They watched as he tousled Stephen's hair, and Megan shot Cathy a sideways look. 'They get on very well.'

Cathy watched them for a moment, and then looked away. 'Yes, they do.'

'It worries you, doesn't it?'

Cathy met Megan's clear blue eyes. 'You're very perceptive.'

'Not really, but you're easy to read.'

She gave a short, mirthless laugh. 'Max doesn't seem to be able to read me. I keep telling him I'm not interested, but he won't give in.'

'Perhaps becuse he is reading you right — because he knows you *are* interested.'

Cathy looked away. 'I'm not — not in what he has to offer, anyway.'

'I'm not sure Max is aware of what he does have to offer,' Megan said enigmatically. 'Perhaps you ought to give it a try. You might be surprised.'

She laughed. 'Not as surprised as Max!'

He must have heard his name because he turned his head and eyed her searchingly.

'What about this tea, then?' he said after a moment. 'Aren't you wenches going to wait on us?'

'Good idea,' Sam said with a grin, and Tony Fry stretched out on the rug and sighed.

'Sounds fine to me.'

His wife kicked him gently in the side. 'You — go and help Max get the tea. It's a man's job to hunt for food.'

The two men grumbled good-naturedly to their feet and set off towards the pavilion, Stephen in tow.

'Lovely looking boy,' Sue Fry said with a smile. 'You must be very proud of him.'

'Yes, I am,' Cathy admitted, following the little group with her eyes.

'He seems to get on well with Max — have you known him long?'

And here we go again, Cathy thought. I wonder if she'll tell me he's stinking rich.

It was a few days before Megan Carver made it into the surgery to see Cathy, and after the midwife had taken all her details and done the weights and measures bit Cathy took her into her surgery and sat her down.

'So, how's it going?'

Megan shrugged. 'Sam's had the scan, which showed no evidence of any further tumours, and the oncologist is quite happy to put him on radiotherapy — apparently the tumour was a seminoma, whatever that means.'

'Just the type of cancer. Some respond to radiotherapy, some to chemo. So, it looks good.'

'Maybe.' She shrugged defeatedly.

'It makes you very aware of your own mortality, doesn't it?' Cathy said gently.

'I lie awake at night and watch Sam sleeping, and I wonder how long I've got him, or if I'll die first, and what of. Does that sound very morbid?'

'Not at all,' Cathy shook her head. 'It's perfectly natural. I expect Sam's doing the same thing. You ought to talk to him about it, try and find out how he feels. He may not want to worry you—like you don't want to worry him, but at some point in your lives you're going to have to face it, and it's ten times easier if you can do it together.'

Megan gave Cathy a thoughtful look. 'You really seem to understand what we're going through.'

Cathy's laugh was a little strained. 'Yes, well, let's just say I've been there.'

'Of course, you've lost your husband! I'm so sorry, I'm so wrapped up in Sam I'd completely forgotten. Did he die of cancer?'

'No—multiple sclerosis. He was thirty-two. It was diagnosed at the same time I found out I was pregnant.'

'Oh, God—but I thought—isn't MS very slow?'

'Not always.' Cathy smiled sadly. 'Sometimes it can be very quick. Michael died after only two years.'

'How dreadful. How did you cope, being pregnant and knowing your husband wasn't going to live to see your child grow up?'

Cathy laughed ruefully. 'To be honest, I didn't have time to notice that I was pregnant. The first time I really paid very much attention to it was when I was in labour, and at that point Michael was in hospital with an infection. I was visiting him, and sitting by the bed rubbing my back because it ached when a nurse came up and told me I ought to get myself up to maternity unless I wanted to have the baby there.' She chuckled. 'He was born two hours later.'

'I bet Michael was thrilled.'

Cathy's smile became fixed. Actually, Michael had

been too ill to take more than a fleeting interest in his son. She felt a familiar shaft of sadness and was cross with herself because after all this time it shouldn't still hurt as freshly as it had then.

'Yes, he was—delighted,' she lied, and turned the conversation firmly back to Megan and her baby.

She was still feeling a little raw half an hour later when she finished the antenatal clinic. Scooping up the notes, she took them back into the office and found herself alone with Andrea.

After a few moments she became aware of an almost physical animosity, and turning towards the practice manager, surprised such a look of hatred that she almost flinched.

'Why can't you leave him alone?' the woman said in a voice that shook with anger. 'I always thought all the comments about sex-starved widows were rubbish, but I can see now that they aren't. You just want him because he's good in bed, but he'll soon get bored with you and your son. He needs a young woman who can keep up with him and he loves me, I know he does. Find someone else to scratch your itches and leave Max to me!'

Cathy was stunned, not only by the totally unprovoked attack, but by the hatred that Andrea obviously felt for her.

What had she ever done to deserve it? She had done her damnedest to put Max off, and everybody in Barton—except Andrea!—had been desperately shoving them together, against her wishes, and now this—this mechanical *harridan* was accusing her of using him to vent her sexual frustration! She was suddenly, toweringly mad.

Drawing herself up, she met Andrea's glare with one of her own. 'How dare you? There is nothing between Max and me, I have no interest in him, I have no intention of having anything other than an absolutely professional relationship with him, and anything you may have heard to the contrary is complete and utter fabrication. You might ask yourself, though,' she continued rashly, 'why it is that if he loves you so much he's spent the past two weeks trying to get me into his bed!'

And with that she turned on her heel and marched out — straight into Max's chest.

He raised an eyebrow. 'What was that all about?'

'Ask her yourself,' Cathy snapped, and, collecting her bag and jacket from the kitchen, she made her way out to the car park and drove home, fuming.

Her mood wasn't improved by Delphine telling her that her mother had been taken ill and she would have to go home.

The rest of the evening was spent on the phone arranging flights and booking a taxi to drive Delphine to Heathrow, and by the time Max appeared at the end of his surgery she was in despair.

She had stuck a note on his door saying she had to speak to him urgently, and she had just tucked Stephen into bed when she heard Max run up the iron steps and pound on the door.

She opened the door and he strode in, looking all round for signs of disaster. 'What is it, what's happened?'

'It's Delphine ——' she began.

'Delphine?' He looked puzzled, then relieved. 'I thought it was Stephen. What's wrong with her?'

'Nothing—her mother's ill, and she's had to go home.'

'Is that all? I thought it was something dreadful from your note!'

'Well, it *is* dreadful!' Cathy exploded. 'How can I work when there's no one to look after Stephen after school or when I'm on call? I can't ask Joan to drop everything and come and live up here miles from her friends, and I don't know anyone I can call on at short notice and then I won't be able to do my job and you'll be right and I'll be a damn nuisance and you'll have to pick up the slack and I was so determined it was going to work—and on top of all that, that vile bitch called me a sex-starved widow!'

His brow creased. 'Delphine?'

'No—Andrea! She hates me, and I haven't done anything to her, and it's all your fault, and now you're going to be all virtuous and "I told you so" about this and I can't cope any more!'

And with that she dropped on to the settee, put her head on her knees and burst into undignified tears.

After a second of stunned silence the settee creaked under Max's weight, and his arms, warm and firm and comforting, wrapped around her and he pulled her gently on to his lap.

'Oh, Catherine,' he said softly, 'you really are in a mess, aren't you, sweetheart?'

And that really was the last straw, because Megan and Sam had brought it all back and she thought again how unfair it all was that she had had to cope alone for so long, and all the hurt she'd bottled up for so long came pouring out all over the front of Max's unsuspecting shirt.

CHAPTER SIX

AFTER a few minutes Cathy struggled to a sitting position and fumbled in her pocket for a tissue.

A large snow-white handkerchief appeared in her hand, and she blew her nose vigorously and scrubbed the tears off her cheeks.

'Sorry, I don't know what came over me,' she said unsteadily, and clambered inelegantly off his lap to go and stand by the window, arms wrapped round her waist, racked with humiliation.

He came up behind her and rested his large, warm hands on her shoulders, pulling her gently back against his chest.

'Want to talk about it?'

She shook her head. What was there to say? It was perfectly obvious that she couldn't cope, without beating the thing to death.

'Have you eaten?'

She shook her head again. 'No, I couldn't ——'

'Nonsense. Come down with me and I'll cook you a meal — Agnes will have left something out for me, and I'm sure it'll stretch. She always overfeeds me.'

'What about Stephen?'

'We'll leave the communicating door open — in fact, let's go down that way.' He led the way to the door and she followed, her mind still in a daze.

Penny greeted them ecstatically, and her good-natured enthusiasm did a lot to restore Cathy's opinion of herself. At least not everybody hated her!

'Steak?' Max asked from the depths of the fridge, and she shrugged.

'Really, Max, I'm not hungry.'

But she was, and as he flash-fried the onions and steak and tossed the salad she found her tummy rumbling appreciatively.

'Still not hungry?' he said with a wink, and she laughed a little shakily.

'OK, you win, but don't give me much.'

In fact she was surprisingly hungry, she found, and quickly demolished the plateful Max gave her, even finding room for a little slice of strawberry flan to round it off.

After they had eaten, Max topped up her wine glass and led her to the sofa in the corner, tipping Penny off on to the floor.

Settling himself into the corner so that he was half turned towards her, he regarded Cathy steadily over his glass. 'OK, let's have it. It's more than Delphine, isn't it? Is it Andrea?'

'No — oh, she's a pain, but no, it isn't her.'

'So who, then?'

She swirled the wine in her glass, worrying her lip with her teeth.

'Michael,' she said finally. She lifted her shoulders in a helpless gesture. 'I was talking to Megan Carver — she came in for her first antenatal check, and I found myself telling her about Michael and how we found out about his MS when I was just pregnant.'

'Did it bring it all back?' he asked gently.

She sighed. 'In a way. You know, it's funny the

things you remember. If anyone asked, I would say we had a good marriage, but when Megan said Michael must have been very proud of Stephen, all I could remember was him saying "What about me?". He was so jealous of any attention I gave Stephen, right from when I first found out I was pregnant. Megan said Sam cried when she told him they were having a baby. Michael said the last thing we needed was a — well, I won't repeat his language, but it was awful. If it hadn't been for Joan I don't think I could have coped, and yet before he was diagnosed he was so happy and cheerful and easygoing.'

She broke off, staring into her wine. 'Stephen asked the other day if his father had liked playing with him, and I had to decide between the truth and what Stephen would want to hear. It was very difficult.'

'What did you say?'

She smiled wanly. 'I compromised. I told him I was sure he would have done if he'd been old enough, and maybe he would. At least at the end he made more effort, as if he finally realised what a pig he'd been.'

She fell silent, thoughtful for a moment, and then shook her head. 'He hated being ill,' she said softly. 'He was awful to me sometimes, and then he would apologise. I'd forgotten how difficult it was.'

'So your idol fell off his pedestal.'

'Oh, no. I never idolised Michael, but I think perhaps I justified things because of his illness that really had no justification. No, today I just admitted how angry I am with him for leaving me to cope alone. That was the last thing he said to me, just before he died. "Cope," he said. Just the one word. He was finding it difficult to talk, and everybody said he was trying to reassure me that I would be all right, but to me it just sounded like an order.'

'And you've tried to obey it ever since.'

She gave a rueful smile. 'Yes. And I really thought I could, but I was wrong, wasn't I?'

'Catherine, you're coping fine.'

Her head snapped up. 'No I'm not! Look at the mess I'm in — without Delphine, how on earth am I going to do my job? God knows who I can get to replace her, and, even if I find someone for the days, what about the nights when I'm on duty? And what about the weekends — and it'll be the school holidays soon. What happens then?'

Her voice was rising again, and she clamped her mouth shut and tried to stop her trembling hands from slopping her wine all over the place.

'No problem,' Max said calmly, taking her glass away and putting it out of harm's way. 'Agnes can fetch Stephen from school, and the nights aren't a problem; we can simply leave the door open.'

'And in the holidays?'

'You'll have found someone by then. I'll ask Agnes to keep an ear open. She might even know someone already. Catherine, calm down, it'll be all right.'

'But it's not — it isn't all right! I should be able to do it on my own, without asking for help.'

'I don't recall that you did ask,' he said, 'and anyway, "no man is an island". We all need help from time to time.'

She met his eyes with frank disbelief. 'But why you? After all you've said, why should you bother?'

'Why not? He's a good kid. I like him. Anyway, it was bound to happen sooner or later.'

'But it shouldn't! Why should you have to do that? You said you'd end up picking up the slack, and now here you are, doing just exactly that because my care arrangements have gone wrong! It isn't fair to you, Max, and if you were honest you'd say I shouldn't have taken the job.' She glared at him. 'I'm just waiting for you to say "I told you so".'

He chuckled. 'Give me time; I'll see what I can come up with. Now, if I give you back this wine will you drink it or throw it over me?'

His smile dissolved her fears, and, with a self-deprecating grin, she reached out for the glass. 'I thought you'd be really angry,' she confessed. 'That's why I was so defensive. I'm sorry.'

'No, I'm sorry. I've given you no reason to believe I would be anything other than thoroughly bloody difficult, have I? You've fitted in really well, done more than your share. Sarah was telling me how good you are in the clinics and how much the patients appreciate you, and Sam Carver thinks you're the greatest thing since penicillin. In short, you're a positive asset to the practice, and we can't afford to lose you. That's why I'm prepared to help.' He leant back in the corner of the sofa and raised his glass. 'Cheers, Dr Harris, superwoman of the nineties, medic *extraordinaire*. Your health.'

She felt a slight flush of pleasure touch her cheeks. 'Thank you,' she murmured. 'I'm glad you're pleased with the way I've fitted in, but it doesn't alter the fact that I've failed as a mother.'

A quick frown crossed his brow. 'How have you failed?'

She shrugged. 'Well, if I wasn't working——'

'Hang on a minute. The fact that you have to work doesn't mean you aren't a good mother.'

'Well, you've certainly changed your tune!' she retaliated defensively. 'I thought you didn't approve of working mothers?'

'No,' he corrected, 'I don't approve of women who work for the sake of it, or have children with no intention of being there for them. Presumably when you and Michael decided to have children, you had agreed that you would give up work while they were very young, at least?'

She shook her head. 'We hadn't agreed anything— we hadn't given it any thought. Stephen just happened. I was on the Pill and I had a tummy bug. The next thing I knew I was pregnant. As for me giving up work, I really don't know but I suspect I would have wanted to work at least part-time anyway.'

He raised an eyebrow sceptically. 'Really?'

'Really. Don't turn me into something I'm not, Max. I enjoy my job, and it's important to me. I need it like a fish needs water. I know that.'

'There's nothing wrong with job satisfaction; just because you have to work doesn't mean you aren't allowed to enjoy it!'

She lifted a shoulder. 'But it makes me feel guilty. I mean, I haven't had any choice, but I know that I would go insane stuck at home all the time raising babies and going to toddler groups and coffee mornings and patting cushions, and I wonder how hard I would have tried to be at home more for Stephen if I hadn't enjoyed my job. He needs consistency, continuity of care, and because of my job I've failed to provide that.'

'Rubbish. Who looked after him in Bristol?'

'Joan, when he wasn't at play-group or school.'

'And you—always you, always there at some point in the day, always caring, always making sure everything was all right with his world. Catherine, Stephen is happy and adjusted and perfectly well looked after, and he will continue to be so. He's well able to cope with a change of ancilliary staff, so to speak, so long as you're there whenever you can be.'

'And when I can't?'

'Than I will be—at least until you can make some more permanent arrangement.'

'Max, I can't ask that of you! You have no idea what a commitment a young child is! What about when you go and play cricket, or squash, or whatever?'

'He can come and watch—and anyway, you're only talking about a couple of nights a week and one weekend in three—that's no hardship, is it?'

'Not for me, no, because he's my son, but I don't know how you'll feel about it. You've only seen his good side so far, remember. What about when he has a tantrum and refuses to co-operate?'

Max grinned. 'I'm sure I can deal with a small boy in a snit.'

Cathy raised an eyebrow. 'Oh, yeah? We'll see. Anyway, it won't be for long. I'll have to find someone quickly because of the holidays. They break up in two weeks' time.'

'OK. I'll get Agnes on it in the morning,' he said easily. 'Right, that's that solved. Now, what's all this about Andrea?'

'Oh, God, her.'

'You've really got it in for her, haven't you?'

'Me? I like that! She hates my guts, and it's all your fault!'

'Mine?' His voice rose incredulously. 'How can it possibly be my fault?'

Cathy wriggled back on the sofa, tucking her feet under her bottom. 'She seems to think you're in love with her.'

'Rubbish. I've never given her the slightest indication that I was even interested, far less in love!'

'Have you slept with her?'

He shifted awkwardly. 'Of course not.'

'You mean you didn't sleep?'

'Dammit, no, that isn't what I mean!'

Cathy raised an eyebrow. 'She said you were good in bed.'

He flushed under her candid scrutiny. 'She has a fertile imagination. I can assure you, I haven't made love to her. I kissed her once. It was a mistake. She got a bit—enthusiastic.'

Cathy tried not to laugh. 'The mind boggles.'

He gave a wry grin. 'Yeah, well. . . Never again. But anyway, what's it got to do with you?'

She sighed heavily. 'Because, in company with everybody else in this town, she seems to think we're having a torrid affair.'

He snorted. 'I should be so lucky!'

She flushed. 'Max, please. I mean it, it's getting difficult and embarrassing. Everybody's making snide remarks about me living in the flat or dropping hints about how lonely you are—and if one more person tells me you're filthy rich I'll throw up!'

Max winced ruefully. 'I had no idea I was so newsworthy—and I'm not *that* filthy rich!'

'Oh, no, of course not. Where did you go to school — Eton? Harrow?'

He cleared his throat. 'Winchester.'

Cathy nodded. 'Figures. Tell me, Max, has your mother ever worked?'

He looked slightly shocked. 'Mother? Good lord, no. Well, apart from her charity work and the WI. . .'

'Charity work? You mean one day a week in the Oxfam shop to salve her conscience?'

He chuckled. 'Something like that. Actually, she's coming up for the weekend soon — I'd like you to meet her.'

'I can hardly wait,' Cathy said drily.

He laughed. 'What's the matter — frightened she'll eat you?'

Cathy didn't doubt it, but there didn't seem to be any point in discussing it. She'd just have to try and get out of it when the time came. In the meantime, she had other, more pressing problems — like the way Max was watching her over the rim of his glass. . .

She stood up and put her own half-empty glass on the table. 'I must go. Thank you for the meal, and for offering to bail me out.'

He rose to his feet, looking down steadily into her eyes.

'Stay with me.'

There was no doubting his meaning, and for one heartstopping, breath-stealing second she was desperately tempted. But then reason reasserted itself and she stepped back, shaking her head.

'No — Max, no, please. . .'

His eyes were still locked with hers, trapping her with their endless sapphire depths, and for a long moment he held her gaze, seeming to see right inside her. If he had reached for her then she would have been lost, but he shook his head wryly and closed his eyes, releasing her from the invisible bond.

'Go on, then, if you must.'

She turned wordlessly and ran up the back stairs, closing the door behind her and sagging back against it in relief.

Her knees were shaking, her heart pounding, and deep inside a nameless passion stalked through her, clamouring for attention.

And that was just his eyes! God knows what would happen if he touched me, she thought frantically, and a low moan of longing escaped from his lips.

He was playing with her, stalking and catching her, then letting her go, only to stalk her again. He could easily have persuaded her to stay—one touch would have done it.

And then what?

'Damn you, Max Armstrong,' she whispered. 'Damn you to hell and back for making me want what I can't have. . .'

After surgery the next day she called on Tom Bickers, who was out of the psychiatric unit and back at home, taking a few days' leave to talk things through with his wife.

He seemed much more stable, but he was still clearly depressed, as well he might be, considering the financial implications of his latest lapse.

'Elaine's going to have to have control of all the money, I realise that,' he said heavily, and it was obvious to Cathy that it was a severe blow to his pride to hand over the financial reins to his wife — especially considering his career in accountancy.

However, there seemed little choice, and it was a step in the right direction, provided that their marriage could survive the power-shift. Somehow Cathy doubted it, but she promised them both her support and assistance whenever necessary.

On the way out, she reminded Elaine to come and see her to have an IUCD fitted when her period started, and she closed her eyes and shook her head.

'I can't imagine that I'll ever let him near me again,' she confessed. 'I will come and have one fitted, because you never know what's going to happen, but I sincerely hope I'll never need it.'

How sad, Cathy thought as she drove away, that, feeling like that, she yet felt she had to stay with her husband out of duty. What good would they be to each other? Perhaps it was just a passing phase, but somehow she doubted it.

Max was waiting for her when she arrived back in the surgery at lunchtime.

'Come to the pub for a sandwich,' he invited, but she shook her head.

'No, I have to ring up some au pair agencies and see if I can find someone——'

'Well, now, hang on, because Agnes may have found you somebody — the daughter of a friend. She's got a baby of her own — not married, but a very nice girl, so Anges said, and she's a pretty good judge of character. Apparently she's a patient of mine, but I can't recall her face. She's working in the pub at the moment and her mother's looking after the baby, but Mum's finding it rather hard work, by all accounts, so the girl's having to give up at the end of the month.'

Cathy felt suddenly railroaded. She knew it was unreasonable, that he was only trying to help, but the whole issue seemed to be slipping out of her grasp, all the arrangements made without any reference to her! What if she didn't like this girl? She might be quite unsuitable —

'But I don't know her!' she protested. 'I've never met the girl — Max, I'm not handing my son over to someone I've never met just on Agnes's say-so!'

'Hey, hey, calm down! Agnes hasn't said anything yet, and I thought if we went over to the pub and had a drink and a bite to eat, you could take a look at her without her knowing. That way, if you didn't like her, we could tell Agnes and you're off the hook without the girl ever knowing anything about it. And besides,' he added with a grin, 'a cold beer and a salad down by the river has a certain appeal today, doesn't it?'

The surgery was hot and stuffy, her blouse was sticking to her back, and she was dying of thirst — quite apart from which, if this girl *was* any good. . .

'Oh, go on, then.'

'So gracious,' he said with a grin, and held the door for her.

It was a short walk to the pub, and they found a table in the shade under a willow. As they sat down, a plump, pretty girl of about twenty came up to them with a smile and offered them a menu.

'Hello, Dr Armstrong,' she said cheerfully, and his brows twitched together.

'Judy, isn't it?'

She smiled broadly. 'That's right — fancy you remembering.'

'How's the baby — little girl, am I right?'

'That's it — oh, she's lovely. Such a dear little mite. Best thing that ever happened to me.'

He leant back in his chair and smiled. 'You must be keeping well — I haven't seen you for ages.'

'Oh, yes, fit as fleas. We see the nurse, of course, and the health visitor, but no, we don't need you, I'm afraid!'

They laughed, and she turned to Cathy. 'You must be Dr Harris — how are you settling in?'

She blinked in surprise. 'Does everybody know me?'

'Little town, Dr Harris — everybody knows everybody here. And being as you were together. . .'

She trailed off, embarrassed, and Max stifled a smile and turned his attention to the menu.

'I think I'll have the crab salad, Judy, please, and a low-alcohol lager. What about you, Catherine?'

'Oh — the same, please. Thank you.'

As Judy walked away, Cathy turned to Max with a glower. 'You see? Everybody's at it! We can't move without someone making a comment about us!'

He gave her a lazy smile. 'Does it occur to you that she might have simply put two and two together and realised you're my colleague?'

'Don't be ridiculous!' she scoffed. 'Why should she look embarrassed?'

He shrugged. 'Perhaps she's just shy — but supposing you're right, does it matter? Am I so bad for your image?'

'Yes — yes, frankly, you are! My professional image is very closely linked to how people view my personal and social behaviour, and if they think I've got the morals of an alley-cat ——'

'Ouch! I'm not sure I like being branded the village tom!'

'You probably deserve it,' she retorted.

'Huh! You can talk about people jumping to conclusions — what about you? I'll have you know that I pursue my personal life with the utmost circumspection! And anyway, nobody's been disapproving. They probably think it's rather romantic.'

She snorted. 'Little do they know!'

'I'm insulted — I'm very romantic. Who was the last person who told you your skin was like the petals of a rose?'

'Idiot,' she chided, then laughed despite herself.

'That's better. So, what do you think of Judy? Any good?'

'That's her?'

He nodded.

'Very nice, what I've seen of her. Might be a bit of a gossip.'

He shook his head. 'I don't think so. I think she's just very open and natural. Anyway, as you keep reminding me, we've got nothing to hide.'

'Yet,' she said rashly, and could have bitten her tongue out.

Max lifted his head, meeting her eyes with a searching gaze, and then a slow smile spread over his face.

'Well, well,' he said softly. 'Progress. . .'

After that she was more conscious than ever of being stalked. Every time she looked up, he was watching her, his eyes seeming to read her mind, a knowing smile flickering in their depths when she looked away and then looked back, flustered.

Stephen was settling well to the new routine of being picked up by Agnes, and seemed highly delighted with the idea that Max would be looking after him during the weekend.

Cathy was less highly delighted, because all she could think about was the fact that the communicating door would be open all night, a sort of symbolic lowering of the drawbridge, and she felt desperately defenceless at the thought.

Max was on call on Friday night and did the Saturday morning surgery, and so Cathy was able to play with Stephen in their bit of garden until Max got home and handed her the mobile phone at twelve.

'Are you sure about this?' she asked him worriedly, for the hundredth time, and he rolled his eyes and sighed.

'Trust me, we'll be fine.'

She took Stephen in for lunch, and they had just finished when the phone rang.

She found Max in the garden, stretched out in a sun lounger, his glorious body naked except for those wretched cut-off shorts.

He lifted his head and peered at her, shielding his eyes with his hand. 'Call?'

'I'm sorry——'

'It's all right. Off you go, we'll be fine, won't we, old son?'

Stephen nodded enthusiastically. 'Can we play cricket?'

'He can't take too much sun, with that fair skin—he needs a hat on if he's out in it for long. Oh, and I've put out a spare set of clothes on his bed in case he should need them for anything, and——'

'Would you please just relax and go and deal with the patient? We're fine.'

She hesitated for a split second, then, kissing Stephen quickly, she ran to her car and drove off. The call had been from a woman whose husband was having chest pains, and she didn't like to keep him waiting.

In fact after seeing him she was almost sure it was indigestion, but as he was only in his forties she rang the hospital and had him admitted for a check-up.

'Just to be on the safe side. They'll run a few tests on your heart and send you home with a packet of Rennies, I expect!' she joked as they waited.

The ambulance arrived and removed her patient, and she was on her way home when the mobile phone rang.

This time her patient was a child with an asthma attack, and after treating her with Ventolin she advised the mother to keep her in and close the windows.

'The pollen count's very high today,' she explained, 'and that doesn't tend to help.'

She was almost home when the phone rang again. Someone who had had a sore throat for two weeks had finally decided it was tonsillitis, and needed urgent treatment.

Telling herself it could have been worse — it could have been the middle of the night! — she scribbled the prescription, made an acerbic comment about normal surgery hours, and made her way home.

The place was deserted, and, finally giving in and going up to her flat, she found a note pinned to the door.

'Gone Fishing', it said, and so she took the opportunity to sort out the washing.

She had another call, an elderly lady who'd taken a tumble in the garden, and still they weren't back.

Finally, at six o'clock when she was getting ready to call the police, she heard voices approaching and went to the door, looking down into the garden as Max and Stephen walked towards her across the grass, a mud-splattered and soggy Penny at their heels. They were deep in conversation.

'. . . and the ones with spikes are sticklebacks.'

'That's right. Can you remember now?'

Stephen nodded. "Spect so. Mum won't know, anyway. She's not into fishing and mucky stuff like that — well, she wouldn't be, would she? She's a girl.'

Max glanced up then and caught her eye, winking at her. She suppressed the glad little leap of her heart and smiled what she hoped was a natural smile.

'Brought the supper home?' she asked lightly.

Stephen and Max exchanged a look that spoke volumes.

'You can't eat minnows and sticklebacks, Mum,' Stephen explained patiently, 'but we caught lots and lots, didn't we?'

'We did indeed.'

'Where are they?'

He rolled his eyes at her ignorance. 'You have to put them back — otherwise it isn't fair, just for our entent — entain. . .'

'Entertainment,' Max supplied, with another wink at Cathy.

'Yeah. What's for supper?'

'Nothing till you're cleaned up and ready for bed. Say thank you to Max, please.'

Stephen thanked him with genuine enthusiasm, and Max smiled warmly.

'My pleasure. Perhaps we'll be able to do something else tomorrow, if Mummy doesn't mind.'

'Wow, yeah!'

'We'll see,' she said quickly, before Stephen could escalate a casual suggestion into a guaranteed commitment, and hustled the child upstairs, bathed him and dressed him in clean pyjamas before giving him the sandwiches she had made earlier.

The phone was peaceful, surprisingly, all evening, and so she was almost startled when it rang a little before ten.

Immediately there was a knock on the communicating door, and she opened it to find Max there, casually dressed in jeans and T-shirt.

'Another call?' he asked quietly.

'Yes, I — I have to go.'

'That's fine. Is Stephen asleep?'

She smiled. 'Out for the count — I think you wore him out this afternoon.'

Max grinned. 'We aim to please. I'll keep an eye on him — and don't worry about the door. Just leave it open, and come and go as necessary.'

'Thanks — I'm really very grateful, Max.'

'Forget it, I'm having fun. I don't get to play uncle all that often.'

So she left him and went out, returning at eleven to a quiet house. There was a dim light shining up from the kitchen and another on the landing, but Max didn't appear and Stephen was still sound asleep.

She showered and was just getting ready for bed when the phone rang again; sighing with resignation, she slipped into clean clothes, tied back her damp hair and let herself out quietly.

This call took longer, an elderly patient with pneumonia who refused to go to hospital until he became so frightened by his breathlessness that he finally gave in.

By the time she got home it was almost one, and she went into her room, more than ready for bed.

'Better check Stephen,' she mumbled sleepily, and tiptoed quietly into his darkened room.

'Stephen?'

She listened for the sound of his breathing, but the room was unnaturally quiet. She walked over to the bed, her heart in her mouth, telling herself she was crazy, that of course he was there, he was just under the covers, but he wasn't.

'How odd,' she muttered, and checked her room again and the spare room, then the sitting-room, the bathroom, even the kitchen. There was no sign of him.

'Max must have him,' she told herself, and, hurrying along the landing, she found a room at the far end, the door standing open.

In the light from the landing she could see Max, sprawled on his back in the middle of an enormous four-poster bed—alone. As if he sensed her presence, his eyes flicked open.

'Catherine?'

'Max, I can't find Stephen. He's disappeared!'

CHAPTER SEVEN

MAX threw off the covers and swung his long legs over the side of the bed, reaching for his jeans with one hand and the light with the other.

'Where have you looked?'

'Everywhere — the bedrooms, the sitting-room, kitchen, bathroom —'

Flustered, she dragged her eyes away as he stood up and tugged the jeans over his bare hips, hooking up the zip as he headed for the door.

'You've checked the flat completely?'

'Yes — I thought he must be here with you.'

'No — I haven't heard anything. We'll look again, together. You might have missed something.'

But she hadn't. The flat was deserted.

'We'd better ring the police,' Cathy suggested, her heart in her mouth.

Max's face was grim. 'Come on, we'll check the house first.'

He turned on his heel and ran lightly down the back stairs to the kitchen, skidding to a halt as he reached the bottom.

Cathy cannoned into his back and he turned to steady her, relief written all over his face.

'He's here, with Penny. They're asleep,' he said softly.

Peering round him, she saw Stephen curled up on the old sofa in the corner, one arm flung over the dog.

Penny's eyes blinked open, and her tail wriggled in greeting.

Gently, so as not to disturb Stephen, Max lifted her off on to the floor and then scooped the little boy into his arms. He made a small, sleepy noise and snuggled against Max's chest, and Cathy nearly wept with relief. Her limbs were shaking almost uncontrollably, and she felt physically sick.

'Oh, God, I was so worried!' she whispered.

Max gave a short, humourless chuckle. 'You were worried? I was supposed to be looking after him!'

He carried Stephen up to his room and slipped him carefully under the covers, taking care not to disturb him. Then they left him, pulling the door to behind them, and went back on to the landing.

Max looked at her keenly. 'Are you OK?'

She smiled wanly. 'I am now. I should have thought of the kitchen, knowing how devoted he is to Penny. I'm sorry I woke you.'

'Forget it. I'm just relieved he's all right.'

She gave a strained little laugh. 'Me, too. Oh, Max, I really thought. . .'

He gave a wry grin. 'I know. Can I get you a drink? Brandy, or something?'

She shook her head. 'No, I'm on call still and it's late. I'd better let you get back to bed.'

He met her eyes, and in the dim light she could see desire flare in the cobalt depths.

Her heart began to pound, the blood heavy in her veins as she watched him. He made no move towards her, simply holding out his hand, and after a breathless moment her hand lifted and reached for his.

Still a small gap remained, and still he waited, his hand steady, mere inches from hers.

Her heart was thudding against her ribs, her mouth dry, and she couldn't seem to get her breath. For an age she hesitated, and then, her eyes still locked with his, she closed the gap between them.

Their fingers meshed, and without a word he led her along the landing to his room, leaving the door open slightly so that they could hear the phone, then he drew her close and took out her ponytail band, threading his fingers through her hair and fanning it over her shoulders.

'That's better,' he murmured, and then his hands slid over her shoulders and down the front of her blouse, pausing at the top button.

What am I doing here? she thought wildly, as his fingers slowly, tormentingly unfastened each button of her blouse. When it was undone he started to ease it over her shoulders, but she pulled it back, suddenly assailed with nerves. What if he didn't want her? What if, when he saw her, he changed his mind? And her underwear—my God, she thought, the ancient once-white sports bra and the practical cotton knickers—so much for the great seduction scene he was trying to set! Once he saw them his desire would keel over and pass out, never to recover! She let out a little moan of anguish.

'What's wrong?' he asked softly.

'Turn off the light, Max,' she pleaded.

'No, I want to see you when I make love to you.'

'Oh, Max, no——'

'Oh, Max, yes. . .'

He wouldn't be denied. His fingers gentle but determined, he prised her hands away from the blouse and slid it over her shoulders. Her skirt was next, dispatched in no time, and then he unclipped her bra and eased it off, groaning gently as he cupped her full breasts in his hands.

'Beautiful — so soft,' he breathed raggedly, and, sliding his hands round to her back, he eased her up against him.

How was it, she thought dazedly, that a body so hard and masculine could be so gentle, its every touch a caress?

His skin was like hot satin beneath her palms, and the dense curls on his chest felt like swansdown as he chafted lightly against her. She could feel the tension in him, his body trembling slightly beneath her palms, and that gave her courage somehow.

She ran her hands down his back, savouring the supple feel of muscle beneath warm skin, the deep indent of his spine, the way he sucked in his breath as her fingers curved round his waist and slipped inside the waistband of his jeans, tracing the line of hair that arrowed down from his chest.

He groaned her name and she grew bolder, the rasp of the zip scraping on their nerve-endings and winding the tension even higher, and then she watched, fascinated, as he wrenched his jeans down and kicked them impatiently aside before drawing her back into his arms with a ragged sigh.

'Oh, God, you're so soft — soft and smooth, like silk — Catherine, I want you. . .'

'Oh, Max, yes,' she moaned, and then he was lifting her, laying her gently on the vast bed and coming down beside her, his body warm and hard against her side.

She raised her hand to his face, and noted with amazement that her fingers were trembling almost uncontrollably. Dear God, and he had hardly touched her!

He lowered his head until his lips brushed hers, and a whimper of need rose in her throat.

'It's all right, sweetheart, there's time,' he murmured, and his hand closed, hot and heavy, over one breast. He growled low in his throat and lowered his head, moving so that his mouth could cover the straining nipple, teasing gently before drawing it deeply into his mouth, his thumb meanwhile dragging lightly over its partner.

Sensation shot through her and she arched against him with a little cry of surprise, her fingers digging into his shoulders.

His mouth returned to hers, greedy now, demanding a response she was only too willing to give, and his hand slid lower, delving gently beneath the soft tangle of curls to the moist centre.

Her breath caught in her throat and she bucked against his hand, trembling wildly as he stripped away the remnant of her underwear and moved over her, steadying her with tender words and caresses as he eased gently into her.

She felt the tension peak and then shatter, felt herself unravelling, out of control, and with a tiny cry of alarm she buried her face in his shoulder and clung to him as wave after wave of sensation crashed over her, leaving her weak and helpless in his arms.

She was dimly aware of his cry of release, of the harsh shudders that racked his body, and then with a muttered, 'Too heavy,' he rolled on to his side, taking her with him, holding her close against his chest until his thundering heart slowed and his breathing steadied, and all the time his hands were moving slowly over her, soothing and caressing, gentling her like a wild animal, calming her fears.

After an age his hands stilled, and he sighed and hugged her gently. 'Are you all right?'

'Yes, I'm fine,' she lied, and forced herself to lie motionless in his arms until the rhythm of his breathing told her that he slept.

And then the tears came, hot, scalding tears that slipped down her temples and ran into her hair.

Dear God, what have I done? she thought, her mind in turmoil.

Because she loved him, and nothing would ever be the same again.

The phone rang a little later, while she was still awake, and she wriggled out of his arms and ran lightly down the landing to her flat.

As she was returning the receiver to the cradle, his arms came round her, hard and warm, and pulled her back against his bare chest.

'Do you have to go out?'

She nodded, unable to speak, unable to face him while her emotions were in such disarray.

'I brought your clothes — hurry back, we have unfinished business,' he said softly, and, sliding his hands down to her hips, he pulled her hard against him.

'Max, don't do that, Stephen might wake up,' she said desperately, and with a low chuckle he kissed her shoulder and went back to his room, leaving a dull, unsatisfied ache inside her.

Her patient was a child with appendicitis, who the

mother had been watching for days because he had had
a grumbling pain that came and went.

'I suppose I should have done something sooner — I
hate calling you out in the night,' the woman said
apologetically, but Cathy soothed her guilty feelings.

'You only know with a grumbling appendix when it
flares up, so there was no point calling me before,' she
explained. 'Anyway, I don't mind, I wasn't asleep
anyway.'

She admitted the child to hospital and then drove
slowly home, unable to face Max.

Would he still be waiting for her? It was nearly four
o'clock, and already the sky was lightening.

Deciding it was cowardice but preferring to call it
self-preservation, she tiptoed in and made herself a
drink, then took it out into the garden, sitting on the
steps as she had done before and watching the sun
crawl over the horizon.

Last time she had done that she had felt peace steal
into her heart, but now there was no room for peace
amid the turmoil. Max had seen to that, with his gentle
hands and soft words, coaxing her so that there was no
escape from herself.

She had never known such earth-shaking, shattering
emotions as she had experienced in his arms — had
never even known they existed until last night.

And now she loved him. Oh, she had wanted him
before, had felt the pull that drew them together, but
now her defences had come down so far, there was no
turning back.

The only problem was, she had no idea what Max
wanted from her, and she had Stephen to think of.
Was it fair to expose him to the possibility of heartache

if things with Max should go wrong? Because she was under no illusions. Now their relationship had reached the point it had, Max wouldn't take no for an answer. In fact Delphine's disappearance suited him so well that she wondered for a wild second if he might not have engineered it.

If only she knew where they went from there.

The phone rang again, interrupting her fruitless train of thought.

It was Mrs Hooper about Clair, the little child whom she had visited during the afternoon with an asthma attack. She was having another, more serious one, and so Cathy gave the mother hurried instructions and ordered an ambulance before driving over there, to save time.

When she arrived Clair was panic-stricken and going into status asthmaticus, and the mother was unable to get her to take the bronchodilator from her Nebuhaler, because the child simply couldn't breathe enough to use it.

After one look at the terrified child, Cathy decided to give her an intravenous injection of aminophylline and Valium, so to cut down on the stress she splinted her hand and put in a butterfly, so that the line would be in for any hospital-administered drugs. That done she injected the aninophylline and Valium through the butterfly, and while they waited they played a trickle of oxygen over her face because she was too frightened to tolerate the mask. The injection thankfully worked wonders, and within a few moments the child started to calm, the cynosis began to fade and they were all able to relax a little.

'How long has she had asthma?' Cathy asked.

'Oh, only a few months really. The other lady doctor before you said she might need to see a consultant, but Clair seemed all right for a while and so nothing was done.'

Another example of failing to follow up, Cathy thought angrily.

'Well, I think we definitely need to do something this time, to track down the cause. Have you any idea what might have triggered this attack?'

The woman nodded. 'Perhaps. My husband opened the bathroom window because it was so hot in there, and late in the evening our neighbour cut his grass — it must have stirred up the pollen and it just filtered into her room,' the mother explained. 'We've talked about having air-conditioning — I wonder if that would help?'

'I don't know — maybe, but she isn't going to be at home all the time,' Cathy reasoned. 'I'll see if I can arrange for some tests so that we can find out exactly what triggers it, and then we can decide the treatment. She may need to be on a prophylactic regime — preventative drugs that make her much less likely to have an attack, rather than treating an attack after it's occurred.'

'Can we do that?'

'Oh, yes. Here's the ambulance — let's get her to hospital for now, and then come and see me with her next week and we'll talk about it some more.'

She briefed the ambulance driver, waved them off and made her way back again.

Nearly six, and she hadn't had any sleep at all. She couldn't be bothered to worry about Max, even. If he wanted her, he could have her. She doubted if she would even notice. Exhausted, she went into her flat, stripped off her clothes and crawled naked into bed, falling asleep instantly.

She woke to silence, the particular silence of an empty house. Glacing at her watch, she was stunned to see that it was a little after ten. 'Oh, lord, Stephen,' she groaned, and struggled to sit up.

There was a note propped on her bedside table, beside a beautiful red rose.

In the garden — come and join us when you wake up. Max.

He must have put it there earlier. She buried her nose in the lovely bloom and wondered if he had stood watching her as she slept, as she had lain last night and watched him in the aftermath of their loving. Her head dropped back on to the pillow and she lay for a second, revelling in the knowledge that there was no need to worry.

The sun hadn't yet come round to her room and the sheets were cool against her bare skin. She stretched lazily, absently noting the unaccustomed sensations in her body.

A little stiff, a little sore, but relaxed in a way she hadn't been relaxed for years. Replete. Sated.

Well loved.

She threw back the covers and went into the bathroom to shower, calmer now in the clear light of day. Of course she and Max could work it out. Oh, he hadn't said he loved her, but it was there in his eyes, in the touch of his hands, in the gentleness of his lovemaking.

And he thought the world of Stephen, that much she knew.

No, it would be all right. She was worrying about nothing.

Dressing swiftly, she ran down the steps and made her way to the garden.

Max was sprawled in one of the teak chairs on the terrace, his feet on the table, reading the Sunday papers. Stephen and Penny were chasing each other round the lawn, and the air was heavy with the scent of roses and honeysuckle.

Max looked up, his eyes warm, and came slowly to his feet. 'Hi, sleepyhead. Ready for breakfast?'

She was suddenly smitten with shyness, knowing what they had shared. 'Just coffee, I think.'

'I'll get it, you sit down.' He pulled out a chair for her, much to her relief, because his proximity was doing funny things to her legs.

Sated, indeed! she thought wryly. You only have to look at the man!

He was back seconds later with a brimming jug of coffee and a clean mug, and after pouring hers he topped up his own mug and dropped back into his chair, stretching out his long legs under the table. He was wearing the jeans he had had on the night before, and her heart kicked at the memory.

She reached for the coffee gratefully and took a hefty swallow to steady her nerves.

'OK? You had a hell of a night.'

'Oh, don't. I was rushed off my feet.'

'I noticed,' he teased.

She flushed under his laughing scrutiny.

'You didn't come back.'

'There wasn't really time.'

His eyes gleamed with unholy laughter. 'I don't recall either of us took very long.'

She coloured again, and he chuckled.

'I love it when you blush.'

'I'm not used to morning-after chit-chat,' she said defensively.

'Hmm. I'm glad you brought that up.'

She frowned in puzzlement. 'Brought what up?'

'Morning-after. In the — er — heat of the moment, let's say, I didn't give a thought to contraception. I don't suppose you've got a coil or anything magical like that?'

She stared at him blankly. 'My God — I didn't think! With all the confusion over Stephen, and I really hadn't meant to — well. . .' She floundered to a halt.

'So have you?'

'No — no, of course not. Why should I need to? The last time I made love I was just barely pregnant.'

A tiny shiver of hope ran through her. She had never thought she would have another child, but now ——

'Oh, well, no harm done. I've got some PC4s in my bag; I'll get them for you.' He got up and went into the house, leaving her staring dumbly after him. When he came back, he dropped a small packet on the table and pushed it towards her.

She left it there.

'Well, go on, then — take them.'

'No.'

'What?'

She looked up and met his eyes defiantly. 'No. We haven't even discussed it ——'

'What's to discuss? We made love rashly on the spur of the moment, and forgot to use contraception. Here's the answer. It's simple.'

She took a deep breath. 'Max, I don't want to take them.'

He let out an exasperated breath and ran his hands through his hair. 'Catherine, be reasonable — you could get pregnant!'

'Yes.'

He stared at her in amazement. 'Are you mad? There's no way our relationship is ready for a child!'

Cathy glanced down the garden to where Stephen was playing with Penny. 'There's something you've forgotten, Max — our relationship already does include a child — or don't you count Stephen?'

'No, I don't — not in the way I mean. Stephen isn't mine; I have no commitment to him. I would expect to have a great deal of commitment to a child of my own, and I would expect his mother to, as well.'

She glared at him. 'Are you saying I don't have any commitment to Stephen?'

'You work, don't you?'

She slammed her coffee-cup down on the table, slopping the contents all over her hand.

'Dammit, Max, just a couple of days ago you were telling me it was fine, that Stephen was well-adjusted and I'd done a fine job and was coping wonderfully well, and now you're saying quite the opposite!'

'Catherine, you said yourself you felt guilty, as if you knew you should be doing better — '

'That's not what I said — '

'That's what it amounted to! Anyway, if and when I have a child, its mother will be at home, giving the child proper care and attention, not out at all hours of the day and night leaving the brat with any Tom, Dick or Harry! Tell me, Catherine, if I hadn't volunteered to look after him, what would you have done?'

She watched him in silence for a second, and then snorted. 'So that's what this is all about. I knew it was a bad idea——'

'Just answer the question.'

'All right. I would have rung the au pair agencies, lined up another au pair to look after him and in the meantime I would have paid a locum to cover my evening surgeries and nights on call. If the worst came to the worst, I would have taken him down to Bristol to stay with Joan until something was sorted out——'

'All highly unsatisfactory.'

'Max, I know that, but I don't have a choice!'

'But even if you did, you'd make the wrong one! You said so!'

'I knew it was a mistake talking to you—I should never have trusted you. I knew you'd end up using it against me!'

She stood up, trembling from head to foot, and Max leant over and took her hand, tugging her back down.

'Catherine, don't be silly. This is getting totally out of proportion.'

She gave a short laugh. 'You think so? I think we're just now, finally, getting down to the nitty-gritty.'

But she sat down, mainly because her legs seemed to be turned to jelly and wouldn't hold her any more. Was this really the Max who had held her and comforted her and told her how well she was doing, who had taken her in his arms last night and carried her to paradise? The man she loved with all her heart?

'Catherine, don't do this to us. Just take the bloody pills and be reasonable,' he said tiredly.

'Me be reasonable?' she exploded. 'I like that — just because I don't agree with you! What if I want another child? Did that occur to you? You wouldn't be the first man to be used as a stud!'

He flinched as if she had struck him. 'Don't,' he said softly. 'That isn't what happened between us last night, and you know it.'

'Isn't it? I thought I did know what happened between us, but now I'm not so sure. I thought there was something deep and real and genuine, something that could last, but now I find you don't want a child because you can't handle the responsibility!'

He let out his breath on an angry rush. 'I didn't say I didn't want a child!'

'Just that you wouldn't give it any commitment. Well, if you won't give your own child any commitment, there's precious little chance of you giving it to another man's child, and if you can't make a commitment to Stephen then it follows you won't make one to me, and I don't need that, Max. I *need* commitment, and, if you won't give it, fine. We'll manage without you. You forget, I already have a child, and if I want another I'll have one!'

'It's my child too, and that gives me rights!'

She glared at him. 'It gives you no rights. The only person in all this with any rights is the child. You gave up your rights when you failed to take precautions.'

'Don't be crass! Anybody would think I was asking you to have an abortion!'

'Don't you mean telling?' she snorted. 'It strikes me there's been precious little asking going on round here. You've told me I'm to take the pills — I'm surprised you haven't simply told me to marry you and give up my job, but that would imply a commitment on your part, and as we all know, you aren't interested!'

'You're being totally unreasonable!'

'I'm not being unreasonable! You're an adult, Max. You know the implications of unprotected intercourse. If you're so hell-bent on not having a child, why don't you have a vasectomy and have done with it? Then you can screw who you like when you like and never have any commitment!'

He shot her a filthy look. 'I never said I didn't want a child at some point. If and when the time is right, of course I'll get married and have children, but in that order, and for the right reasons, and to the right person.'

'Meaning I'm not? What makes you think I'd have you anyway?' she said bitterly. 'You're stiff-necked, self-opinionated, over-privileged—God, you make me sick! To think I really thought I could love you!'

She stood up abruptly and ran down the garden to Stephen.

'Come on, darling, we're going back to the flat.'

He tipped up his head and looked at her, disappointment written all over his face. 'Do we have to? Max said we'd be going fishing again this afternoon——'

'He's busy.'

'No, he isn't! He said he isn't!'

She grasped his wrist and all but tugged him up the garden. 'Something's come up. Come on, darling, please.' She was near to tears, her heart in tatters, and as they drew closer to Max he stood up and walked towards them.

'Say "thank you for having me",' she prompted Stephen, refusing to meet Max's eyes.

'My pleasure, old son. We'll do it again some time.'

'Over my dead body,' she whispered under her breath, 'and don't call him your son!' and then she towed Stephen round the corner and up the steps to her flat. Stephen flounced off into his bedroom and slammed the door defiantly, and Cathy went into her room and sat heavily on the bed, her heart pounding. 'Old son, indeed!' she gritted, and, picking up the red rose from the bedside table, she deliberately crushed it in her hands.

A little while later the phone rang, and she had to go out on a call. When they arrived at the bottom of the steps, Max was standing there.

'Leave him, he'll be all right with me.'

'I'll take him. He can wait in the car.'

'Catherine——'

She glared at his fingers, wrapped around her forearm. 'Take your hands off me.'

After a long moment, he sighed and released her, and she hustled Stephen into the back of the car and fastened his seatbelt. Max followed her round to the driver's door.

'Catherine, please. . .'

'You're in my way, Max.'

'We need to talk.'

She met his eyes then, and all the anger and bitterness of his betrayal showed on her face. 'I have nothing—absolutely nothing—that I wish to say to you.'

His face hardened, the features becoming cold and unwelcoming, and he stepped back.

'So be it.'

She got into the car, slammed the door and drove off without a backward glance.

CHAPTER EIGHT

NEEDLESS to say, working with Max became difficult in the extreme, and it wasn't helped by Andrea's evident delight at their rather obvious chilliness towards each other.

They were both icily polite in public, and in private Cathy shed endless bitter tears.

Her row with Max, of course, did nothing to help solve the problem of Stephen's care until she could get an au pair. She spoke to Judy, who said she would be delighted to look after Stephen once she stopped working in the pub, but that wouldn't help at night, and it didn't help for now.

Sunday night had been mercifully quiet, but she had had one night call and was very conscious of Max's disapproval when she got Stephen out of bed and bundled him sleepily into the car.

'What the hell do you think you're doing?' he had asked furiously when she returned.

She had ignored him, sweeping past him up the steps to her flat with Stephen alseep in her arms, and shut the door in his face.

But she couldn't go on doing that, and if she had a night like Saturday night Stephen would be exhausted. Equally, she couldn't ask Max to help her either, and it didn't seem fair to ask Agnes to do any more.

In the end she rang Joan, and she agreed to come up and stay over Cathy's next night on call.

And then on Tuesday her period started, and the whole foundation for their bitter row crumbled, together with her hopes and dreams.

In a way she was relieved, but at the same time something inside her died. She had so wanted another child, and hadn't allowed herself to cherish the dream until it was almost in her grasp.

And now it was gone, shown for the vain hope it had been, and she tried to put it behind her and carry on.

That same morning Mrs Bickers came to see her, light-headed with relief because she wasn't pregnant, to have her coil fitted.

'I know what I said to you, but I love him in my way, and we've shared a lot. Perhaps with time I'll change the way I feel, but I'm never having another child, I know that. It wouldn't be fair. Just thank God for those pills you gave me.'

Cathy made non-committal noises and with the help of Sarah she deftly inserted the IUCD, thus ensuring Mrs Bickers's safety on that front.

'How about the money?' she asked, to change the subject to one less raw on the nerves. 'Have you managed to sort anything out?'

'Well, we've spoken to the building society about remortgaging to include the loan Tom took out, so we can clear that and get rid of that nasty little shark, and I'm trying to get a job in the daytime, but it's hard to get anything to fit in with the school holidays, and I daren't work in the evenings because God knows what Tom would get up to if I wasn't there to watch him all the time.'

'You still can't trust him, can you?' Cathy asked gently.

She snorted. 'Would you?'

Cathy shook her head. 'It would be difficult.'

'It's impossible. You know, you live with someone all those years and you think you know them, and then you find you don't know them at all, that you've been living a lie all that time, but they still expect you to stand by them and bail them out when they get in a mess — oh, well, you don't need to hear all that.'

She stood up and smiled wearily at Cathy. 'Thanks for all your help.'

'You're welcome. Come and see me if you need me.'

She watched her go and then sat thoughtfully for a moment, staring vaguely at the door. Elaine Bickers was right about thinking you knew a person. Cathy had allowed Max's gentleness with her body to cloud her memory of his acidic attitude when she'd first started work here, making her think she had imagined that harsh streak in him. It had come as a shock to discover that the real Max was both men rolled into one, inseparable from each other. Talk about taking the rough with the smooth!

She sighed. Oh, well, perhaps it was for the best that she wasn't pregnant. He would only have been high handed and autocratic about his 'rights'.

Stifling the threatening tears, she pressed the inter-com button and called the next patient.

Max cornered her at home that evening.

'Catherine, we have to talk,' he said firmly, blocking her way when she would have walked straight past him and up the steps to her flat.

'I have nothing to say,' she said, just as firmly.

'Well, I have. Your attitude is ridiculous. How the hell are we supposed to work together when we can't discuss anything?'

She stopped trying to get past him and forced herself to meet his eyes. 'You want to talk about work?'

He glanced down at his hands, then back to her face. 'No. I want to talk about us.'

She squashed the little ray of hope ruthlessly. 'What "us", Max? There's you, and there's me and my son.'

'And the child we might be going to have because of your stiff-necked refusal to see sense ——'

'My what? What about your carelessness, or doesn't that count? Although I suppose I should be grateful to you for that, because without it I might never have realised what a truly ruthless bastard you are!'

He drew in a sharp breath, obviously containing his temper with difficulty. 'Whatever your personal feelings towards me, I can't let you take the responsibility for a baby on your own.'

'Oh, can't you? Well, well. The ghost of a conscience — or were you about to offer me some of your abundant money?'

He compressed his lips into a firm line, his grip on his temper obviously in danger of slipping. 'Damn it, this is hard enough without your snide remarks about my over-privileged background!' he snapped. 'Now, are we going to talk about it or not?'

She gave up. There was, after all, nothing left to fight over.

'There's nothing to talk about, Max ——'

'What do you mean, nothing to talk about? Who's going to look after the baby while you're at work, and how will you afford a proper nanny? You'll have to have time off—there are all sorts of things we need to discuss——'

'What's the matter, Max?' she goaded. 'Worried you'll be saddled with my maternity leave?'

'Damn it, Catherine, will you take this seriously? We simply can't go on avoiding each other and the issue indefinitely——'

'There's nothing to talk about, Max,' she interrupted gently, 'because there is no baby.'

'What?' He stared at her blankly.

'I'm not pregnant, Max. You're off the hook.'

'Oh.' He looked away, clearly stunned, and she could have sworn she saw disappointment in his eyes for a second. 'Well, that's that then.'

'Yes.'

His shoulders sagged slightly, and he turned on his heel and walked slowly away.

A few minutes later Agnes arrived with Stephen, full of beans about the cooking he had done with her since he got home from school.

'We made chocolate crispy cakes—you can have one, I've brought them home—and Stan let me ride on the mower with him when he cut the grass, and we fed the ducks, and tomorrow Agnes says we'll go into town and do some shopping and I can feed the ducks on the river——'

'Darling, Granny's coming tomorrow, so I'll have to talk to Agnes about that. Run along in—here's the key. Can you manage?'

She sent him in with the cakes, and explained to Agnes that she would have the following afternoon off until five-thirty, and Joan would be arriving at about four after Stephen was home from school, so Agnes would not in fact be needed.

'Well, that's a blessing, actually,' the older woman said, 'because I really ought to go and pop in on old Mrs Jones and make her a cup of tea, and young Stephen'd get awfully bored.'

So that was settled without offending anyone, and the following afternoon Joan arrived in good time for Cathy to go off to her evening surgery.

She went into the kitchen to grab a cup of tea before she started, and found Max in there alone. Changing her mind, she was just about to turn round when he looked up and gave a wry smile.

'Don't leave on my account. Actually, I wanted to see you. I'll watch Stephen tonight so you don't have to take him out with you on your calls. There's no reason why he should suffer just because we've had a tiff——'

'Tiff? I would call it rather more than that, Max— and anyway, why the sudden concern? Don't tell me you actually care?'

'Don't be absurd, of course I care,' he retorted. 'If you insist on taking him out with you when I could quite easily keep an eye on him, I think you're being petty and ridiculous——'

'My mother-in-law has come up for the night,' she told him coldly, 'not that my child care arrangements are anything at all to do with you.'

'Oh, for God's sake! There was no need for her to come up. I said I'd cover your on call until you got another au pair, and I meant it. I honour my commitments, Catherine.'

'Oh, I'm sure you do,' she said sweetly. 'The difficulty is getting you to make them. Now if you'll excuse me, I have patients waiting.'

She took her tea with her, only realising after she reached the sanctuary of her room that she had forgotten to take out the teabag and hadn't put any milk in.

'Damn him,' she said, well aware that she was being unfair but past caring. She threw the tea down the sink, fished out the teabag and put it in the bin and plonked down with a sigh behind her desk.

If only she weren't so tired! What she needed, of course, was a decent night's sleep, but every time she lay down her thoughts turned to Max, and that wasn't precisely conducive to relaxation.

She had two calls to make immediately after surgery finished, and when she got home Joan took one look at her before sending her to lie down.

'Catch a bit of sleep while you can. I'll wake you before I put Stephen to bed so you can say goodnight, and have a bit of supper.'

She nodded obediently and went to bed, only too grateful to hand over the reins for a while at least. Not that she expected to sleep, but it would be wonderful just to lie down. She slipped off her dress, pulled the quilt up and fell asleep the second her head touched the pillow.

Joan woke her at eight, and she kissed Stephen goodnight and went into the kitchen.

There was a chicken salad laid out, and some sparkling grape juice, and because it was light and because Joan had gone to some trouble to prepare it, and because in any case her body if not her mind was ready for food, she forced it down almost automatically.

Then Joan herded her into the sitting-room, closed

the door and sat her down on one end of the sofa, taking the other end herself.

'Right, tell me.'

Cathy smiled wanly. 'I can't hide anything from you, can I?'

Joan's answering smile confirmed it. 'Max?'

She sighed. 'Yes, Max. I've been a fool, Joan. I let myself believe he could love me, and that he would take to Stephen, which he has, of course, but not to the extent of wanting any kind of a commitment.'

'To Stephen, or to you?'

'It's rather one and the same thing, isn't it? If he can't make a commitment to my child, what good is that to me?'

'You could always have an affair.'

Cathy felt the tears prickle behind her lids. 'I don't think so. It hurts enough after one night, without making a habit of it.'

'Oh, dear.' Joan leant forwards and put her hand over Cathy's, squeezing gently. 'Not premeditated, I take it?'

Cathy almost laughed. 'You might say that. Joan, I don't know what to do. Every time I see him, every time I hear his voice, my heart just stops. I'm so angry with him, but I love him so much. . .'

She pressed her fist to her mouth to hold back the sobs, and, with a motherly clucking noise, Joan gathered her into her arms and rocked her gently.

'Oh, Joan, I feel such a fool,' she said after a while.

'Is there really no hope?' Joan asked, so Cathy told her about their row on Sunday morning.

'Well, you know,' Joan said reasonably, 'I can see

his point about not wanting to start a relationship with the burden of a child——'

'But he knows I've got a child! He's known that right from the beginning, so it's a bit late to use that as an excuse. No, Joan, he just wanted an affair, and as soon as there was any possibility it might be more than that he wanted out. I should have realised he would. No good-looking, normal, healthy man is still running around footloose at thirty-four unless that's the way he wants to be—particularly not one with that much money!'

'Unless he just hasn't met the woman he's been waiting for.'

Cathy gave a strained little laugh. 'Well, take my word for it, it isn't me! He wants a nice gently bred little debutante with big boobs and a stay-home mentality to raise his heirs in the manner to which he's been accustomed, not a middle-aged, raddled old hag with stretch marks and somebody else's son!'

Joan stared at her in amazement. 'Are you sure the hang-ups are all on his side? It sounds to me as if you've got a bee in your bonnet about his money, and if he's inherited it it's hardly his fault, and on the subject of middle-aged, raddled old hags, it doesn't exactly seem to have put Max off—are you sure you don't need a new mirror?'

Cathy looked away. 'Don't be daft, Joan, I don't need you bolstering my ego with image-propping clap-trap. I know how I look, and what I am. All I ask is to be left alone to live my life in peace. I didn't want to fall in love with Max, but now I have and he doesn't want me and——'

'Has he said he doesn't want you? Have you actually given him a chance to say what he feels?'

Cathy snorted inelegantly. 'Oh, don't worry, he made his feelings perfectly clear—he's nothing if not articulate. Must be the expensive education.'

Joan tutted reproachfully. 'Catherine, really, you're getting so bitter. I always did worry about you after Michael died, but I thought that when you finally met the right man you'd come to life again. Instead of that you're eaten up with self-pity and bitterness.'

Cathy met her mother-in-law's eyes with horror. 'Oh, Joan, is that how I seem? I'm sorry. I'm just not very good at being rejected.'

'I know—and so you create this image of yourself that makes you undesirable, and tell yourself that nobody could want you, and that saves you having to go out there into the real world and compete for some man's attention. The trouble is, when you get a man's attention for the first time in ages you don't know what to do with it, and it's such a shame, because it would do you good!'

She gave a rueful chuckle. 'Max would laugh to hear you say that. He's been telling me the same thing for weeks.'

'Well, has it occurred to you there might be something in it? Perhaps you ought to accept what he's offering at face value and just enjoy his attention for a while.'

Cathy sighed heavily. 'Oh, Joan, if only. The trouble is the price I would have to pay for his attention is far too high. I'm not that kind of person. I can't just have an affair with someone because it would be fun. I get much too involved, and I need all the things he can't or won't give me. Anyway, it isn't fair on Stephen. I didn't realise before how badly he needs a father figure, but he's coming to rely on Max, and I know he's going to get hurt.' She sighed sadly. 'I wish Michael hadn't died. We were happy before he was ill. I'm sure we could have made our marriage work.'

Joan shook her head. 'You can't change the past, Cathy.'

'Well, God knows I don't seem to be having much luck with the present or the future! Oh, Joan, I just don't know what to do. All I know is every day is agony, seeing him and knowing that he doesn't love me. . .'

She stood up and walked to the window, staring down sightlessly into the garden. 'I'm not sure how much longer I can stand it. If I hadn't slept with him, I could have put my feelings on the back burner and ignored him, but now. . . He was so. . .kind and tender—gentle, as if he really cherished me. I felt so needed, so loved, so wanted. And then in the morning—oh, Joan, it was awful! I couldn't believe what he was saying!'

Joan stood up and walked over to her, laying a sympathetic hand on her shoulder. 'If it all gets too much, Cathy—if you feel you need to get away, you can always come and stay with me and do locum work until you find something else. Don't be afraid to admit you've made a mistake and come home.'

It was Joan calling it home that did it, because it made Cathy realise just how much she thought of Barton-Under-Edge as home now. Everywhere she went, people recognised her and said hello or gave her a friendly wave as she drove past. Megan Carver could very easily become a friend, and Sarah had asked her round for a meal one evening. Stephen had found a friend in Ricky and Delphine had often had the other little boy over to play after school, and Cathy had even seen a little terraced cottage near the river which had a For Sale board outside. She had meant to go and see the estate agent and find out how much it was, but now. . . Oh, yes, she had made a mistake — the mistake of putting down roots. It would break her heart to leave, but how much more would it hurt to stay?

'This is my home now,' she said bleakly. 'I can't think of Bristol as home any more. I love it here, and I'm just beginning to make friends. I just wish you were a bit nearer so I could pop in for coffee like I used to. I miss that. At least you know what I'm talking about and I don't have to pretend with you. No, I think the thing to do is to move out of his flat and get another au pair, and just keep my distance from him. Once I've got a circle of friends it won't be so bad. I'm sure I fell into his bed out of loneliness as much as anything.'

'Hmm,' Joan said non-commitally, and Cathy gave her a wan smile.

'You don't agree.'

'No, I don't. He's had a profound effect on you from the first time you met him. I think blaming it on loneliness is ducking the issue. You love him, Catherine, and if you imagine keeping yourself busy is going to take that away I think you're fooling yourself.'

The phone rang, giving Cathy a legitimate escape from what was fast becoming a tricky conversation. It was a busy evening after that, and she didn't have time for any further self-indulgence.

'Thank God you were here, I couldn't have dragged

Stephen out that many times,' she said tiredly to Joan in the morning.

'It was the least I could do — and don't forget, if you need to come, the door's always open.'

She thanked her old friend with a lump in her throat, and then left, dropping Stephen at school on her way to the surgery.

Max followed her into her room.

'Can I have a word?'

She sighed. 'Is it important?'

'I don't know, but I'll try not to waste your time,' he said with a trace of sarcasm. 'It's about Clair Hooper.'

'Clair — what about her? She's asthmatic.'

'Yes, she's coming in to see you this morning. I just pulled out her notes. You saw her on Saturday afternoon and again during the night, and I see you admitted her in the end. She's one of my patients, but the mother asked specifically for you. I just wondered if there was anything I ought to know.'

Cathy shrugged. 'Apart from the fact that Pauline failed to refer her to a hospital consultant when the problem arose a few months ago, not really. I think she needs looking at so we can track down the cause, but there may be more than one thing. I expect her mother wanted to see me because I suggested a follow-up.'

'Hmm.' He perched on the edge of her desk. 'Any ideas?'

She pursed her lips and shook her head slowly from side to side. 'No. I don't know what the hospital will have come up with, but I wondered if it could be grass. There were a lot of lawns being mowed on Saturday, and it was very still.'

'But it started in February, so it can't just be grass.'

'No, that's what I thought. I'll ask her if she can think of anything that happened in February that might have triggered it.'

'They've moved at some point — we've got a change of address registered on the notes. If it coincided, it might be worth looking at the carpets.'

'Carpets?'

He nodded. 'Apparently wool carpets shed dust-mite allergens much more freely than synthetics, possibly because of the lack of static trapping the dust. There was something about it in the *Lancet* a while ago.'

He stood up and dropped the notes on her desk. 'I'll look it out for you. I've probably still got it somewhere.'

Cathy felt suddenly rather churlish. 'Max?'

He stopped at the door and looked back.

'Thank you.'

A fleeting smile touched his lips. 'You're welcome.' He opened the door and started to go out, then turned back. 'About Friday night.'

'Friday?'

'You're on duty. Is Joan coming up again?'

Cathy sighed inwardly. 'No, she can't, it's her night for the Samaritans.'

'What will you do with Stephen?'

She looked away from him. 'I thought I might ask Ricky's mother if she could have him for the night.'

'Oh — right. Well, let me know if he can't stay there. I was just going to say my offer still stands.'

And now she was truly confused.

'Max, I really think, in the circumstances——'

'Oh, to hell with the circumstances,' he said shortly.

'You can't drag the poor kid in and out of bed. If you can't sort anything out, I'm quite happy to look after him. OK?'

She met his glare with difficulty. 'OK—and thank you.'

He grunted and left her.

Well, what was she supposed to make of that? Was it because he really cared about Stephen, or was it just his wretched sense of honour that made him stick by his offer?

Damned if she knew, but one thing she did know— she wished he would make up his mind and stop blowing hot and cold!

Mrs Hooper was able to confirm that they had moved into their new house just a few days before Clair had had her first asthma attack, and yes, the carpets in the sitting-room and in Clair's bedroom were wool mixture. The carpets in their previous house had all been polypropylene or Antron, and that might well account for Clair's allergy. In fact, Clair had been helping with the housework on Saturday when her first attack had occurred, and closing her bedroom window might have exaggerated the problem on Saturday night.

The hospital had made arrangements for a whole battery of tests in the Outpatients' department, but in the meantime she had been discharged on twice-daily Becotide, an inhaled corticosteroid in powder form. They had found she needed to use it more at night, which seemed to bear out the carpet theory, but she found the powder difficult to inhale. Cathy suggested Mrs Hooper should move Clair into a different bedroom for a while, with polyester pillows and duvet, and keep her out of the sitting-room during the evening, and she switched the Becotide for Pulmicort, a fine liquid spray form of corticosteriod which she could inhale from her spacer more easily.

'If she shows no improvement, let me know,' she told the mother, 'but I think you may find we have the cause, or at least part of it.'

And Max, of course, had thought of it. She found the article on her desk on Friday morning, with a note from Max.

> Hope this helps. M.

She saw him later and related what Mrs Hooper had told her.

'It fits with the contents of the article.'

He nodded. 'Does seem to. Oh, well, we'll watch her and see, and report to the paediatrician. How are you fixed for tonight?' he asked then, with an abrupt change of subject.

Not very well, was the short answer. 'I'm still trying to get hold of Ricky's mother,' she stalled.

'Well, you know where I am,' he said briefly, and went out on a call.

By that evening she was forced to admit defeat and ask him to keep an ear open for Stephen.

'He'll be fine, don't worry,' Max reassured her, and Stephen seemed only too delighted by the arrangement.

It was another hectic night, and she woke in the morning to find a note from Max—this time outside her bedroom door.

> Agnes has a cold, so I've taken Stephen into town with me. See you after surgery. Max.

There wasn't time before surgery to get aggravated by his latest take-over bid, but as she finished up with the last patient and headed home she was starting to seethe.

She found them in the garden. 'You should have woken me and told me, not left a note! He's my child, and I have responsibility for him, not you!' she raged.

'Oh, God, I might have known I'd done the wrong thing,' he said wearily. 'There's no pleasing you, is there? Either I won't take responsibility, or I take too much. You want to make up your mind.'

'My mind? I like that! Who is it that has the problem with commitment?'

He sighed and shook his head. 'Catherine, I have no problem with commitment——'

'No, because you simply avoid it!' Stephen was playing on the grass with the dog, as usual, and she called him over.

He came bounding up, bursting with life and enthusiasm. 'Hello, Mum. We've made all sorts of salad for lunch, and Max bought some funny pink fish that's all see-through and smells disgusting, but it's lovely—Max, what's it called?'

'Smoked trout.'

She could feel herself being engineered. 'Who said anything about lunch?'

Max shrugged. 'We all have to eat, and it seems to make sense to do it together. Anyway, preparing it passed the morning, didn't it, chum?'

Stephen nodded enthusiastically. 'I had some of the pink stuff, and some of Agnes's homemade soda bread, and there were some funny little baby tomatoes.'

'Cherry tomatoes,' she said absently. 'Max, really, you shouldn't. . .'

He shrugged again, diffidently. 'I wanted to talk to you, quietly without interruptions. I thought if we had lunch and then took Stephen and Penny for a walk by the river, we'd be able to sort something out.'

'But, Max, there's nothing to sort out——'

'Later,' he said softly. 'Stephen, how about coming and helping me bring the things out? You can start by giving your mother a drink.'

They reappeared a few moments later, Stephen slopping a tall glass of something clear and fizzy which turned out to be gin and tonic, and Max with a groaning tray full of delightful looking canapé-type nibbles. He put the tray down on the table with a flourish.

'*Voilà, madame*. Lunch is served.'

She sighed and sat down, resigned. 'Thank you,' she murmured mechanically, and tried to make herself concentrate on the food. It was delicious, but she found her eyes straying constantly to Max's long tanned legs. He was wearing a pair of tailored shorts today, and looked as devastatingly attractive as ever.

No wonder I gave in to him, she thought despairingly. Having the attention of a man like that was very flattering, but she told herself she should have had the sense to see it for what it was.

She bit into one of the cherry tomatoes absently, and the juice dribbled down her chin and dripped on to the front of her blouse.

'Damn,' she muttered, but then Max's hand was there, napkin held in his long, lean fingers, dabbing at the stain on her breast.

'I'll do it,' she said breathlessly, and snatched the napkin from him, scrubbing frantically at the mark.

'Will it wash out?'

'I expect so.' She handed back the napkin, and as he took it his fingers closed over hers, trapping them. She looked up, startled, and met his eyes, shocked at the desire that shimmered in their depths.

She snatched her hand back as if she had been burnt, and then scolded Stephen for trying to sneak food under the table to Penny.

'I tell you what, why don't we take Penny for a walk now?' Max suggested, and Penny dashed up to Max, whining and wriggling her tail, tongue lolling, eyes bright and eager.

'Anybody would think you know what a walk is,' Max said to the dog, and she bounced round his feet, tail lashing furiously.

'Come on, we'll go down the garden and over the wall,' he said, and Cathy got reluctantly to her feet.

'Am I all right like this?'

She was wearing a pair of culottes and flat pumps with her tomato-stained blouse, and Max nodded. 'It's quite dry, and there aren't any nettles. You should be OK.'

They made their way down the garden, Penny and Stephen running ahead, and Cathy waited for Max to start whatever it was he had to say.

However, he didn't seem to be in any hurry, and Cathy was damned if she was going to provoke what could only be an unpleasant conversation. He helped her over the wall and then led the way down through the fields to the bottom of the valley where the river wound its lazy way towards the town.

Penny was already in the water and Stephen was on the bank pulling off his shoes and socks.

'Mum, take my shoes,' he yelled, and waded in after the dog.

Max scooped them up with his fingers and left them there, dangling in his hand as they strolled along the shady path. 'It's only shallow, he'll be fine,' Max assured her as she glanced back anxiously. 'Here, let's sit down.'

There was a fallen tree across the path, and they sat on its smooth surface, Stephen's shoes between them marking the great divide.

Max glanced at them and gave a bitter chuckle. 'Symbolic, don't you think?'

'Max, it isn't Stephen.'

'No.' He looked up at the boy, splashing happily in the river with the dog. 'No, you're right.' He let out his breath on a heavy sigh, and looked across at her. 'I still want you, you know. My nights are haunted by the memory of your body under mine, so warm and soft, and the funny little noises you made——'

'Max, stop it!' She covered her ears, her cheeks flaming, and tried frantically to banish the images he had conjured in her mind.

'Catherine, for God's sake, can't we work something out? Just because I didn't propose to you after one night doesn't mean I don't care.'

'Oh, I know you care, but so do I.' She turned to face him and made herself meet his eyes. 'As soon as I realised just how much, I knew it was a mistake. That's why I didn't come back. I needed time to think about what I'd done, because I was so sure I'd been a fool, but then you left me that rose, and I thought maybe —

who knows? Perhaps we could make it work. But I was wrong, wasn't I? You don't want a long-term, permanent commitment, and for Stephen's sake as well as my own I can't settle for anything less, so there we are — stalemate.'

'That's crazy,' he said softly. 'You still want me — I know you do, I can tell by the look in your eyes. We were good together, Catherine. Give us a chance.

'A chance for what? For you to indulge your selfish whims?'

'That's unfair,' he chided. 'It was far from one-sided, and I don't recall leaving you unsatisfied.'

Catherine flushed and turned away. 'No, well, it wouldn't sit well with your ego to do that, would it? Anyway, that's quite beside the point. I'm not going to have an affair with you, Max, and if we're going to continue to work together you'll have to accept that. There's a house for sale in town that I'm thinking of having a look at, because all these cosy little lunches and breakfasts are going to have to stop. You're getting too close to Stephen and he's beginning to rely too much on your company, and anyway I can't cope with you trying to talk me back into bed all the time, it just ins't fair. If you can't keep your distance, then I'll have to leave.'

'Leave?' He sounded shocked. 'Catherine, you can't!'

'I can, Max, and if necessary I will. I warned you right from the very beginning that I didn't want an affair, and you wouldn't take no for an answer. Well, this is your last chance.'

He stood up. 'OK. If that's the way it has to be, then so be it. I can't let you drag Stephen away from Barton when he's settling in so well, and God knows you're needed in the practice, so I shall spare you any further exposure to my "selfish whims".'

With a mocking bow, he turned on his heel, whistled to the dog and set off up the fields, leaving her alone with Stephen.

'Where's Max gone?' he asked.

'He's busy. I tell you what, why don't you see if you can show me those fish you were on about?'

She slipped off her shoes and waded into the water beside him, and hand in hand they stood in the river, watching for minnows, while Cathy told herself that it couldn't hurt for ever. After all, she'd got over losing Michael. Losing Max couldn't be any worse, could it?

CHAPTER NINE

FOR the first few days Cathy was optimistic. Max was polite but distant, refrained from all attempts to talk her into continuing their relationship and otherwise generally kept out of her way. Her nights on call he covered as before, and, although one night she found Stephen curled up with the dog as he had done that fateful Saturday night, Max slept through her retrieval of her sleepy son and was fortunately none the wiser. It was, however, a less than ideal situation and she redoubled her efforts to find an au pair before Stephen broke up for the summer holidays at the end of the week.

She also went to see the estate agent handling the sale of the little terraced house she had seen, and discovered that although it was more expensive than she had hoped it was in every other way ideal for them. The best thing about it was that it was already vacant and the agent thought she might even be able to rent it from the owners, pending completion of the sale.

She viewed it with Stephen, put in an offer and sat back to wait for the result. Well, hardly sat back. The surgery was abnormally busy, with the hayfever season at its height.

On the Thursday morning Max came to see her.

'I had to go out to Clair Hooper in the night. She was having another asthma attack — God, it was a humdinger. I thought we were going to lose her.'

'Really? I thought the hospital were taking care of her?'

He shrugged. 'They don't seem to be able to get to the bottom of it. I don't think she should come home again until they've got her stabilised and settled on an adequate prophylactic regime. She can't keep doing this, poor kid.'

Cathy remembered the little girl's terror. 'I wonder if physio would help her to control her panic? I'm sure that's half her trouble.'

'Oh, at least. I gave her some aminophylline and Valium IV, and she settled very quickly, but by the time I got there she was in a hell of a state already, and I didn't hang about.'

Cathy had heard his car roar off the drive during the night with a great splattering of gravel, and had wondered what the emergency was that had lit such a fire under him. Now she knew.

'I wonder why she seems to have been all right for so long?' Cathy pondered.

Max shrugged. 'Who knows? Perhaps the housework with Mum triggered the first attack this time, and now she's hypersensitive. That coupled with fear of another attack would probably be enough. If she wasn't that sensitised before, it's quite possible she could have had a quiet period. Her mother had been feeling unwell for a few weeks and so hadn't done the vacuuming quite as often, so perhaps there was just more dust about to become airborne on that day.'

'Perhaps. It's a great shame it wasn't followed up months ago. Of course, if you'd been as conscientious about checking on those of your patients who were seeing Pauline as you are those who see me, it *would* have been picked up.'

Max regarded her thoughtfully for a moment. '*Touché*. I take your point. However, I didn't realise it would be necessary to follow up on her every action until later in the year.' And then with an abrupt change of tack, he asked, 'Have you found anyone to look after Stephen in the holidays yet?'

She shook her head. 'No. I asked at the school. One of the mothers is short of cash and could look after him just until Judy finishes at the pub. She's going to think about it and let me know.'

A swift frown creased his brow. 'Won't that be very unsettling for Stephen?'

'I don't have a choice, Max. Stephen knows her, and Judy seems a nice enough girl. Anyway, I'm going to try and get a new au pair lined up — oh, and I think I've found a house.'

'Yes, Sam told me.'

'Sam?'

'Sam Carver. He's a partner at the estate agency.'

'Oh. Small town.'

Max smiled wryly. 'Yes, it is. He wondered why you were moving out.'

Cathy looked down at her fingers, twisted together until the knuckles were white. She took a deep breath and made herself relax.

'Did you tell him the truth?'

'What, that I'm a heartless bastard and didn't want to bring an unwanted child into the world?'

Her head shot up and she glared at him. 'Speak for yourself! I wanted it!'

'Yes, you made yourself clear on that point.' Max

turned away, his jaw working. 'No, I simply told him that you wanted to get into property. I also told him to mind his own damn business.'

She swallowed. 'Thank you. How is he?'

'Oh, OK. Hating the radiotheraphy to bits. He's feeling fairly sore and a bit sick, and generally exhausted, but apparently the oncologist is very pleased with him and the radiotherapy is just a safety net. They're confident that there was no spread of the tumour and the prognosis is excellent. Megan's coming to see you, by the way. She's horrendously morning sick, apparently.'

'Probably worry. So was I. I'll try and talk her out of having drugs—perhaps some relaxation exercises will help.'

But when Megan arrived, it was obvious that she was in a very bad way.

'I can't even keep water down,' she confessed. 'I just feel totally exhausted, and every time I move I feel worse.'

Cathy picked up the skin on the back of Megan's hand and released it. It stayed put, in a papery fold, only slowly sinking down.

'Megan, you're getting very dehydrated. If it gets much worse you'll have to go into hospital on a drip to replace your lost fluids and correct your electrolyte balance.'

'But I can't do that!' she cried, clearly horrified. 'Sam needs me.'

'Yes, he does—fit and well, and so does your baby. How do you feel about drugs?'

'Oh no. No, Cathy, I couldn't. I just feel. . .if

something went wrong with the baby, I would feel guilty for the rest of my life.'

'OK.' Cathy gave up on that tack, because in any event she agreed with Megan. 'Right, well, we'll have to tackle it from the other angle. Have you tried sucking ice-cubes?'

'Ice-cubes?'

Cathy nodded. 'Also try fizzy water—carbonated mineral water, soda water, that sort of thing, all very cold, and sip it slowly. Pressed English apple juice—the cloudy stuff, you know? Once you're keeping water down, that might help you improve. Slices of cold, peeled apple, and plain boiled rice, with salt on. And don't cook for Sam, and don't let him cook anything smelly. Tell him to make himself salads and eat them in the garden!'

She gave a weary giggle. 'I can just see how he'll react to that!'

'Megan, I mean it. You're on the brink of what's known as hyperemesis gravidarum—roughly translated, over-the-top sickness of pregnancy. We have to take it seriously. If you don't improve within forty-eight hours, you're going to have to go to hospital whether you like it or not. How many weeks are you now?'

'Ten.'

'Right. You've got another two, maybe four weeks of this, gradually diminishing, and once the placenta takes over the function of hormone production at fourteen weeks things should improve dramatically. That's the best thing about pregnancy,' Cathy said with a grin. 'It is, by definition, a self-limiting condition!'

'Thank God!' Megan said with feeling. 'Oh, well, at least I can empathise with Sam and his radiotherapy.'

Cathy smiled sympathetically. 'I should have thought it was more the other way round, myself. I'm glad things are going so well for him.'

'Touch wood.'

Cathy eyed her keenly. 'You're still worried, aren't you?'

'Well, I don't know—you hear of so many people dying of cancer, it's a bit like being on Death Row, isn't it? You know it'll happen, but you just never know when, and the longer it takes, the worse it must be, because your hopes get higher.'

'Megan, I think his chances are very much better than you imagine. From what Max was saying, the oncologist is quite satisfied that they've got it licked.'

'Oh, well, I hope so.' She swallowed, and looked around a little desperately. 'Cathy, I'm sorry. . .'

She dashed for the sink and retched helplessly for a few seconds, then collapsed back into the chair, shaking. 'Oh, God, I just want to go home. . .'

'How did you get here?' Cathy asked her.

'I drove.'

'Do you want me to ring Sam and get him to come and take you home?'

'Could you?'

'Yes, of course.' She picked up the phone, dialled the number Megan gave her and passed on the message.

'He'll be here in a few minutes. Will you be all right in Reception while I finish my surgery?'

She nodded and stood up shakily. 'Thanks, Cathy.'

'My pleasure. I'll pop in and see you later, and see

how you're doing. I want to keep an eye on you for the next couple of weeks.'

She watched Megan go, noting how much thinner she was than she had been. Poor woman. What with Sam and the baby, she was being torn in half. And if Cathy knew nothing else, she knew how that felt.

A few moments later the phone rang, and, excusing herself to her patient, she picked it up.

'Dr Harris.'

'I've put Megan Carver in the treatment-room to lie down—what the hell were you thinking of, making her wait in Reception?'

Cathy took the phone away from her ear and looked at it in disbelief. Perhaps she ought to tie a knot in his neck so that he could remember the things he'd said!

'House rules, I thought,' she said with acidic sweetness.'

'Oh, don't be bloody daft! I expect you to use your initiative!'

'I thought I did that last time!' she snapped, and crashed the receiver back on to the hook, seething. 'Now, Mr Jenkins, where were we?'

She caught up with him later in the kitchen, and launched straight into the fray.

'How dare you?' she began furiously. 'My relationship with you is quite fraught enough without you moving the goal-posts every thirty seconds!'

'And hello to you too.' He hefted a mug in his hand. 'Coffee?' he said mildly.

'Don't tempt me, I might throw it over you,' she retorted, and, turning on her heel, she stalked out with as much dignity as she could muster. Damn the man! She went out on her calls, came back and signed a pile of repeat prescriptions under the unforgiving eye of Andrea the Android, and, because she was desperately conscious of Max's voice drifting from the kitchen, she knocked over a cup of tea on the prescriptions and Andrea had to run them all again.

'And that's lost me all my Brownie points,' she muttered under her breath as the enraged Andrea tackled the computer. For once it decided to misbehave for her, and Cathy stifled a smirk and crept quietly back to her surgery.

By the time she had finished her antenatal clinic, resigned the prescriptions, done her evening surgery and gone home, she was emotionally drained.

She met Agnes and Stephen on the drive. 'I have to go and see Mrs Carver,' she told Stephen as they walked back to the house. 'Can you bring something to look at in the car while I go in and talk to her?'

'Oh, Mum, do I have to?' he wailed.

'Yes—please, come on, darling. It won't take long. Perhaps we can go and get fish and chips on the way home.'

'I want a McDonald's.'

She sighed. 'There isn't one in Barton, Stephen——'

'Then why don't we go somewhere else?' he asked mulishly.

'Because I don't have the time or the energy or the desire to, that's why! Now come on——'

'No! I don't *want* to! I want to stay here.'

'Well, you can't. Now get in the car, please, and stop making such a fuss.'

Stephen pouted and kicked at the gravel. 'I want to stay with Max,' he said sulkily, sliding a sideways look at Max's car whch had just pulled up in front of the house.

'No. He's busy. Now get in——'

'You always say he's busy now, but he never is! You just don't want me to be friends with him! Well, just because you don't like him doesn't mean he's busy!' he argued with unassailable logic.

Cathy wasn't in the mood to listen to logic, however. 'Stephen, stop doing that in your school shoes and get in the car, please. Now!'

'Problems?'

She glared at Max, who was strolling towards them, hands in his pockets.

'Nothing I can't handle.'

'Mummy won't let me have a McDonald's because she can't be bothered, and she won't let me stay with you because she doesn't like you any more, and I hate her!'

And with that, he burst into tears, much to Max's astonishment and Cathy's total chagrin.

'Stephen, pull yourself together and get in the car!' she all but shouted.

Max laid a hand on her arm and shook his head gently. 'Hey, hey, don't yell at him. This is more than it looks. Do you have to go out?'

'Yes, I do, I said I'd go and see Megan Carver this evening, but the little tyke won't co-operate——'

Max sighed. 'Leave him with me. Go and see Megan, and I'll see if I can get to the bottom of this.'

She looked down at Stephen's hunched shoulders as he huddled into Max's side, and felt a wave of despair.

'Go on.'

With a shrug, she got into the car and drove away,

glancing back to see Max crouched down to Stephen's level, in earnest conversation. Oh, well, she couldn't worry about it now.

She arrived at the Carvers' house, a smaller version of Max's without the outbuildings, and Sam opened the door to her and ushered her through to the drawing room at the back. There Megan was lying on a settee, looking pale but less drawn than she had earlier, and there was a little bowl of ice-cubes in front of her.

'How's it going?' Cathy asked gently.

'Bit better, touch wood. The ice-cubes seem to help, and I even kept down a little bit of rice. Not much, but I suppose it's a start.'

'Good. You're looking better already. Just try and relax as much as possible, and let Sam run round after you.'

He groaned laughingly. 'Don't encourage her! She's bad enough.'

Cathy smiled at him. 'I'm sure you can cope. You're looking better, too.'

'Yes, I'm OK today, but I've got another clout of radiotherapy tomorrow which will screw up the weekend, I have no doubt!'

'At least it's available.'

He nodded thoughtfully. 'Mmm. Oh, by the way, while I think of it, they accepted your offer on the house, and they're quite happy to rent it to you once you've exchanged contracts, but I'm afraid they won't let you move in before that in case it all falls through and they can't get you out. It's a pity, it'll mean a few more weeks at Max's, but I don't suppose it's any hardship being forced to stay at Barton Manor!'

Not much, she thought wryly. She made a non-committal noise, said goodbye to them both and went back to the delightful and strife-torn Barton Manor to find out how her son was coping with getting his own way. It was a wonder Max hadn't dumped him in the Mercedes and whisked him off to Cheltenham to a McDonald's!

She found them on the terrace, in the process of putting beefburgers on a barbeque.

'Home-made Big Mac,' Max said with a grin.

'Don't you mean a Big Max?' Stephen offered.

Max groaned. 'Listen, you, you've got too much energy. Run into the kitchen and find the ketchup and the butter from the fridge.'

They watched him go, and then Cathy turned to Max. 'Well?'

'He doesn't want to move. He said he hates the new house because it's got a tiny little garden, and he won't be able to play with Penny, and then in the end——'

He broke off and looked uncomfortable.

'Yes?'

'He said he'd miss me.'

Cathy sat down at the table and put her head in her hands. 'I knew it. I just knew this relationship would cause problems. He's latched on to you because he's missing his Granny, and now I'm taking him away from you, too. It just makes me the ogre. He's lost his father, his grandmother, Delphine, you, and of course he'll be looked after by Judy instead of Agnes—when will it end?' she asked despairingly.

Max sat beside her and covered her hand with his. 'Now can you see why I don't like the idea of working mothers?'

She snatched her hand away. 'But I don't have the choice! What else can I do?'

He shrugged. 'Part-time? Locum work to coincide with school terms only? There must be ways round it.'

She bit her lip worriedly. 'I thought once he was at school it would be easier, and I really believed that being out in the country would be better for us both, but perhaps I should have stayed working part-time in Bristol and not tried to buy a house yet. Perhaps I'm just being greedy, but I wanted to be able to give him all the things other children have.'

There was a pause, and then Max said quietly, 'Perhaps the most important thing you could give him that other children have is his mother.'

She met his eyes for a long, anguished moment, and then nodded. 'I think you're right. I'll talk to John Glover, and take him back to Bristol to Joan. I'll have to work my notice, and then there's the contract on the flat——'

'To hell with that. John will let you go now, if you really feel you must, and I don't care about the flat. I'll tear up the agreement. I only let it because it seems a shame to have it standing empty when there are homeless people about.'

She could feel tears forming in her eyes, and blinked them away. 'He breaks up after school tomorrow. I'll take him home at the weekend. Will you be able to get a locum at such short notice?'

Max nodded. 'There's an old boy in the town, semi-retired, who usually does our locum work. He's very good. I'm sure we can get him to cover.' His eyes met Cathy's, and she could see genuine sadness in them. 'It's a great shame. I'll miss you.'

'Oh, Max, don't. . .'

She lost the battle with the tears, and they slipped down her cheeks and splashed on Max's hand as it held hers on the table.

'Is Mummy crying because you burned the burgers?'

She sniffed and dashed the tears from her cheeks. 'No, darling, I'm just a bit tired. Stephen, how would you like to go home to Granny?'

He eyed her doubtfully. 'With you?'

She ruffled his hair. 'Of course with me.'

'Can we go to the park, and McDonald's and all that stuff?'

She nodded. 'I expect so.'

His face lit up. 'Great. Is Max coming?'

Max and Cathy exchanged a look.

'No, darling. Max has to stay here and look after all his patients, and Penny needs him, too.'

'How long will we go for?'

Cathy took a deep breath. 'Forever—to live.'

Stephen looked from one to the other, and leant against his hero.

'What about Max?' he asked.

'I'll come and visit you sometimes, if you like,' Max suggested, his arm round Stephen's shoulder.

Stephen was looking doubtful again. 'Will you bring Penny?'

'If you want me to.'

'I'll miss you,' he said, his lip wobbling perilously.

Max swallowed hard. 'No, you won't—you won't have time, with all the trips to the park and all those Big Macs your mummy'll buy you.'

'I will,' he said quietly.

'I'll miss you, too, old son,' Max said gruffly, and

wrapped his arms around the little boy, hugging him hard. Then he let him go and stood up, clearing his throat hard. 'OK, how about these burgers?'

She saw very little of Max the following day, although he had obviously spoken to John Glover. John was sympathetic and as helpful as possible, insisting that she should leave as soon as she was ready.

'I've contacted Brian Miller and he's able to take over from Monday, so you get yourself off as soon as you like, my dear. I'm just only too sorry it hasn't worked. You've had such bad luck, losing your au pair like that and not being able to get anyone else. I suppose in Bristol it was easier?'

'It was. There were always agency girls I could call on in an emergency, and of course my mother-in-law was nearly always available. She had Stephen every time I was on call and at the weekends, and I just hadn't realised how much she helped until she wasn't there.' She paused. 'I'm sorry I've let you down. I was really enjoying working here, and the people have all made me so welcome.'

Except Andrea, of course, but she kept that to herself.

John nodded. 'They've all spoken very highly of you. It's most unfortunate.' He sighed heavily. 'I suppose in a way Max was right. If you'd had a husband as back-up, your nights on call wouldn't have been such a problem. I don't suppose you'd consider staying and getting on-call cover from a locum agency?'

She shook her head. 'It wouldn't be fair on the patients, John. They're entitled to expect continuity of care. Anyway, there are personal reasons, too.'

'Max?'

She nodded.

'Oh, dear, I am sorry. I hope it wasn't my meddling?'

It was partly, of course, but she hadn't the heart to tell him that, and anyway she and Max had been set on an emotional collision course from the first moment they met.

There was no sign of Max when it was time to go, but John came out of his surgery to say goodbye.

'You will make sure that Elaine and Tom Bickers get adequate support, won't you?' she said worriedly to him. 'Don't let them slip through the net, John. Tom's making such an effort, and Elaine is at the end of her tether. I just feel if we drop them now they'll lose all chance of getting back on top.'

'Don't you worry, my dear, we'll look after them. Good luck.'

Andrea couldn't even be bothered to keep the smile off her face as she said goodbye, and Sarah didn't work on Fridays. She left a quick note on her desk, and then went and collected Stephen from school, laden down with all his bits and pieces, box models and pasta pictures and paintings mounted on black sugar paper, and they took one last walk down by the river before going back to pack and have supper.

There was no sign of Max, and when she got up in the morning his car was gone. She wasn't sure he had even been home, but when they went down to the car with the essentials, she found a beautiful, sweetly scented red rose lying on her seat. The note said:

I hate goodbyes. I hope things work out for you both. Keep in touch. Max.

She stuck the rose on the dashboard where she could see it, and piled all the luggage into the boot, sniffing hard. Then, with one last look round, she started the car and drove away.

CHAPTER TEN

IT WAS her favourite time of day, and Cathy sat in
Joan's little town garden, turned her face up to the last
rays of the sun and tried to ignore the roar of traffic.
Even here, in what was definitely a residential area,
she was endlessly conscious of the background noise.

She sighed. Life in Barton had been so peaceful, a
little oasis in her life, despite the emotional turmoil of
her time there. Short-lived though it had been, she
missed it as though it were the only home she had ever
known, and coming back to Bristol was the hardest
thing she had ever done.

Even her son, desperate for McDonald's and Pizza
Hut and the park and the swimming-pool, had said
today that he didn't like Bristol any more.

'Can't we go back, Mummy?' he'd pleaded, but she
knew they never could.

Max hadn't been, of course. Stephen talked about
him constantly, asking almost every day when he would
come, and it was hard to tell him that Max was too
busy when the truth was he simply didn't care enough
to bother.

God, why did it still hurt so much?

She stood up and paced restlessly round the garden,
absently dead-heading the roses and tugging up the
odd weed. She'd better not let it run away with her
while Joan was on holiday.

She had been a real brick, jollying them both along

when Cathy was ready to throw herself in the river, and looking after Stephen for odd days while she did a little locum work to stoke the coffers.

It had given her a valuable breathing-space, time to rebuild her relationship with her son and try and sort out her feelings for Max — although they defied sorting. In fact, there was nothing to sort. She loved him, pure and simple. It was as easy and as difficult as that.

Dropping the weeds on the compost heap, Cathy glanced up at the back of the house. Stephen was in bed already, complaining of a headache and feeling sick. She ought to go and check on him, although she knew it was only too much sun. They had spent the day at Weston-Super-Mare, just down the estuary, playing on the beach and eating ice-cream, and, although she had tried to keep his sun hat on, there had been times when it had fallen off and she hadn't noticed.

Oh, well, he'd be better tomorrow, and maybe it would teach him to be more careful in future. She went in and ran lightly up the stairs, to his bedroom at the back.

She knew something was wrong the moment she opened the door. He was crying softly, almost moaning, and he had been very sick.

'Oh, darling. . .'

She lifted him carefully out of bed and took him through to her room, noting as she carried him that his little body was burning up with fever. As they went into her room, he moaned and turned his head towards her, and then when she put him down his hands came up and covered his eyes.

'Too bright,' he sobbed.

She closed the curtains and went back to him, her heart in her mouth. Nausea, vomiting, fever, headache, photophobia——

'Oh, God, no, please not meningitis,' she whispered. She stripped off the messy pyjama jacket, noting as she did the bruising-type rash that seemed to be spreading over his body under her eyes. She sat him up gently and said, 'Can you just tuck your chin down on your chest for me, there's a good boy?'

Her heart pounding, she waited as he tried to bend his neck, but he couldn't do it, whimpering with pain and gingerly lying back against the pillows, his head turned from the light.

'Mummy, my head hurts,' he moaned, 'I want Max.'

She smoothed back his hair, kissed his burning little cheek and stood up. 'You lie there quietly for a moment, darling. I'm just going to get you something to make you feel better.'

Running downstairs, she retrieved her carefully ordered medical bag with the neat array of drugs all set into pockets in the foam lining of the lid, and ran back upstairs.

Pulling out the benzylpenicillin, she checked it twice. She would give him three hundred mg IV. She flicked a glance at Stephen, and noticed that he was grey and clammy, mumbling under his breath and moaning softly. There was no doubt in her mind, he had meningococcal meningitis.

Her heart was racing, but she took a steadying breath, splinted his wrist and inserted a butterfly into his hand, then injected the antibiotic, all the time talking reassuringly to him. He was unaware of her now, slipping deeper into unconsciousness under her very eyes.

Trying hard to stay calm, she went into Joan's bedroom, picked up the bedside phone and rang the hospital, telling them what she suspected. They arranged for his immediate admission, and said they would send an ambulance. She quickly gave them the address and ran back to Stephen, who was vomiting again. The ambulance seem to take ages but in reality took only minutes to arrive, and then they were winding through the streets, lights flashing, siren blaring, while Stephen lay lifeless on the stretcher.

They were met on arrival and wheeled swiftly to a dimly lit isolation ward on Paediatric ITU, where they were greeted by nursing staff gowned and masked and ready for action.

A doctor appeared, similarly clad, and after a swift examination he decided to perform a lumbar puncture.

'I think you're almost certainly right,' he said quietly, 'but we have to do this as back-up. I'm sorry.'

While the nurses prepared Stephen for the lumbar puncture, Cathy filled the doctor in with the little information she had about the sudden and unheralded onset of the illness while he scrubbed up at the sink in the corner.

'It all fits,' he agreed. 'Thank God you got the benzylpenicillin into him so promptly. OK, are we ready?'

The nurses nodded, and he looked at Cathy.

'You staying or going? He won't enjoy it.'

She swallowed hard. 'I know. I'll stay, he'll need me.'

She sat beside the bed, one hand holding Stephen's,

the other gripping on to the rail of the bed, while a nurse wrapped one arm around his knees and the other round his shoulders and curved him firmly round, ignoring his weak moans of pain.

To give the doctor his due he was as quick as possible, but, by the time he withdrew the lumbar needle and they lay Stephen flat at last, Cathy was almost sick with reaction.

She tried to stroke his head but he groaned and turned away, and so she sat beside him, holding his hand and biting her lips, while they connected the IV drip to the giving set she had already put in.

The doctor laid a hand on her shoulder and gave it a comforting squeeze.

'All over,' he said reassuringly. 'We're running in the antibiotic now, but I'm going to get the lab technician out of bed to stick this under the microscope and do a Gram's stain to see if he can identify any bacilli. As for Stephen, it's just a case of watching him for any changes. The next forty-eight hours will be critical. There'll be a nurse with him at all times, and the nursing staff will bring you something to eat and drink whenever you ask. I'll write you up for some rifampicin as prophylaxis. OK? I'll be back soon with the result.'

She nodded numbly, her eyes fixed on her son's damp, grey little face. It seemed unreal to be sitting there, watching him slip further and further into the grip of the fever and being powerless to help him. The nurses came and went, always at least one in the room at any given moment, and always gowned and masked beyond recognition.

Stephen mumbled and fidgeted in his sleep, frequently asking for Max, and at one point slipped into a coma which brought the doctor back post-haste.

'Is he going to die?' she asked calmly.

'I hope not,' he replied, just as calmly. 'It is meningococcal, as we thought. You know the risks as well as I do. You caught it early, but we just can't tell at this point which way it will go. Just keep talking to him quietly, so he knows you're here. That'll hold him if anything can. Who's this Max he keeps asking for?'

Who, indeed? 'A friend of ours — an ex-colleague,' she said after a moment.

'Can you get hold of him?'

'What, now? In the middle of the night?'

The doctor shrugged. 'It might help. Might help you, as well as Stephen. You could do with some moral support. Feel free to use the phone in Sister's office.'

She thanked him numbly and turned back to Stephen. He was conscious again, just barely, and asking for Max.

'I want him, Mummy,' he mumbled. 'Where is he?'

'He's asleep, darling, it's night-time.'

'Will he come in the morning?'

She bit her lip. 'Maybe.'

The little boy drifted off again, and Cathy stood up stiffly and went to the window, staring sightlessly into the night. The sky was lightening. Soon it would be dawn.

Could she ring him? He did say he'd come, she thought. Perhaps she'd try later. If only she could get hold of Joan, but she was on Crete with her friend from the Samaritans, and Cathy had no way of contacting her.

The hours seemed to pass in a blur, with nurses and

doctors coming and going, and Stephen slipping in and out of consciousness. At one point his temperature spiked alarmingly and there was a flurry of activity, but then he stabilised again.

At five-thirty she decided to call Max. She had struggled against it, but every time Stephen woke he mumbled his name, and finally she couldn't bear it any more.

She waited until six, then slipped out into Sister's office and dialled his number, and then waited and waited and waited until an electronic voice told her that there was no reply, and cut her off.

'He must be there!' she thought in despair. Where else could he be at six o'clock in the morning?

In someone else's bed, was the short answer. Shocked at the sudden, stabbing pain, she stumbled back to Stephen's room and dropped into the plastic-covered armchair, defeated.

She tried again at seven, in case he had been in the shower or had gone out for a run, as he sometimes did, and then again at eight, and then at eight-thirty she rang the surgery and got Andrea.

'He's on holiday,' she was told brusquely, and was promptly cut off. She rang back, asked to speak to John Glover and asked him if he had any way of contacting Max.

'He's at home, as far as I know,' John said. 'Can I get him to call you?'

'It doesn't matter,' she said heavily, and hung up. Oh, lord, help me, she thought, I can't cope any more on my own! Where are you, Max?

She walked slowly back to the little room, blinded by tears, and saw a large man bending over the bed,

holding Stephen's little hand in his own much larger
one. He was gowned and masked, with a cap on, and
as she went in he straightened and turned towards her.
The only thing she could see of him was a pair of
dazzling blue eyes above the mask, and then she found
herself enfolded in strong, tender arms that held her
against a rock-solid and painfully familiar chest.

'Max?' she whispered in disbelief.

'Shh. It's all right, I'm here. I've got you.'

'I tried to ring—I've been trying for hours,' she
sobbed.

'Hush, darling, it's OK now. Come on, sit down.'
He led her to the chair and pushed her into it, perching
on the arm and wrapping his arm firmly round her
shoulders.

Stunned, she leant against him. She had wanted him,
and he had come—but how? 'How did you know where
to find us?' she asked eventually.

'I didn't. I woke up in the night and I couldn't get
back to sleep. I just had this terrible feeling that
something was very wrong. I even tried to ring you at
five-thirty, but there was no reply.' He shrugged
expressively. 'You could have been anywhere, but it
seemed unlikely. Anyway, I had the day off and it's a
nice drive. I decided to come down and see if I could
find you. I arrived just after seven, and there was your
car in the drive, bedroom windows open, and no
answer at the door.'

He gave a wry chuckle. 'Your neighbours probably
think I'm the local cat burglar, but I shinned up on the
porch roof and climbed in through the bedroom
window. One look round and it was obvious Stephen

was ill, so I telephoned all the hospitals and finally tracked you down.'

'And here you are.' She reached up and touched his face, still unable to believe he was real, and he caught her hand and pressed a kiss against her palm.

'Here I am, as you say.'

She let out her breath on a weary rush. 'Thank God.'

'So, how are things? I had a hell of a fight to get in here, and they insisted I wear all this rubbish. Then one of the nurses asked me if I was Max, and then it was all right and they couldn't get me in here quick enough.'

'He's been asking for you—over and over again. I told him you were alseep, but when I tried you at six and you weren't there, I didn't know what to say to him. But he hasn't said anything since then——' She broke off, too upset to speak, and Max just held her quietly while she struggled against her tears.

The doctor who had been on all night came in then, and checked Stephen's condition on the chart.

'I gather you're Max,' he said with a wry smile. 'You've been very much in demand, I'm glad you got here.' He turned to Cathy. 'He seems to be holding his own at the moment, Dr Harris, but it's still early days. We should have a better idea tomorrow night.' He shot her a worried look. 'Why don't you try and get some sleep now? There's a room next door you can use. We'll wake you if there's any change.'

She shook her head. 'No, I—I couldn't leave him. Please, don't make me!'

Max squeezed her shoulder. 'Nobody's going to make you do anything. I tell you what, if I get you a blanket and a pillow, how about curling up in that chair and having a few minutes? I'll watch him for you.'

She was too tired to protest, her nerves too tautly stretched for any further confrontation. Max tucked the pillow under her head, pushed her back against it and covered her gently with a soft white blanket. As he lifted her feet on to a chair and tucked the blanket round them, she mumbled, 'You will wake me, won't you?'

She didn't even hear the reply.

She slept for nearly two hours, during which time Max kept watch over them both, his brow etched with worry. Stephen seemed to be shrinking before his very eyes, and Catherine—God, Catherine had practically faded away in the five weeks since he'd seen her. Her soft curves were gone, leaving only planes and angles in their place, and her face was white and drawn, the freckles standing out like sentries across the pale skin.

He glanced across the room at her, his face softening. God, he'd been such a fool. All that talk about marriage one day if he found the right woman, and she'd been there all the time, under his nose. He'd just panicked, thinking she might be pregnant, and then when she'd said she wasn't—the disappointment had caught him broadside. He'd been stunned, but the damage to their relationship had been done, and no amount of fancy footwork seemed about to convince her to take him back.

And to think he'd been afraid of commitment! Hell, he might have known he was committed to her anyway after that night. His gut clenched at the memory. So much love, so much tenderness—he'd never felt like that before, never felt that pleasing his partner was the only purpose of the exercise.

She'd struck a chord, of course, when she'd told him that his pride wouldn't have permitted him to leave her unsatisfied, but it was far, far more than that. 'Cherish' was the word that sprang to his mind, and he rolled it round, savouring it.

Stephen moaned and moved restlessly on the bed, and Max crossed to his side, bending over and speaking softly to him.

'Max?' His little eyes fluttered open, and Max felt such a welling of love inside him that it threatened to overflow.

'Hello, old son,' he murmured gruffly. 'How are you doing?'

'My head hurts,' Stephen whispered, his voice a mere thread. 'Don't go.'

'I won't. Don't worry, I'm staying right here with you and Mummy.'

With a contented sigh, Stephen slipped back into the grey half-world of semi-consciousness.

Max stayed beside him, emotions flayed raw. 'Get better, damn you,' he muttered fiercely under his breath. 'Don't leave me now, just when I know how much I love you. You hang in there, old son, you hear me?'

A nurse brought him a cup of coffee and he drank it absently, his eyes locked on Stephen.

Catherine stirred and sat up, and he gave her the last of the coffee.

'How's Stephen?'

'He woke up and recognised me. He seems pretty stable.'

Her shoulders drooped in relief, then tightened again. 'It's still early days.'

'But the signs are good.'

She nodded vaguely, watching Stephen, and Max felt his heart twist at the love in her eyes. God help him, once this was over he was going to do everything in his power to win her love, because without it he was nothing.

The day dragged, an endless succession of doctors and nurses and technicians. Some of them Cathy recognised, some were new. All were unfailingly kind and gentle with both her and Stephen, and behind it all was Max, strong, solid, a rock to lean on—but for how long? Dared she lean on him? For now she would allow herself the luxury, because she needed him too much to fight it, but later—later didn't bear thinking about.

He disappeared for a while and came back with some sandwiches and coffee which he made her have while he stood over her, and later he produced a bar of chocolate and shared it.

She took the rifampicin when he handed it to her, noting absently that he was taking it too, and after a while she curled up in the chair again and slept for a while.

When she woke it was dark outside and Max was slumped in a chair on the other side of the room, fast asleep. As she straightened his eyes opened and he looked directly at her, and her heart flip-flopped in her chest.

'OK?' he asked quietly, and she nodded.

He stayed there, on the other side of the room, and

although she would rather have had him beside her she didn't know how to ask.

There was no change throughout the long night or the following morning, but around noon Stephen became more restless, his state of consciousness changing until finally, at about four, he woke up properly for the first time. Cathy could have wept with relief, and the doctors started being cautiously optimistic.

By six it was obvious he had turned the corner, asking for a drink in a funny, croaky little voice. His headache was receding slowly, and the drink stayed down, much to Cathy's relief.

At nine he fell into a deep, normal sleep for the first time, and the doctor actually smiled.

'I think he's going to make it,' he said confidently. 'Why don't you go home and have a bath and something to eat and a few hours' sleep in a proper bed, and come back in the morning? I think he'll probably sleep right through, but if he doesn't we can always ring you and you can come straight back.'

She was about to protest, but Max agreed with the doctor and before she knew where she was she was being whisked out to the car park and driven home.

He handed her the house keys which he'd found on the hall table where she'd left them, and then while she cleaned her teeth and soaked in the bath he cleared up the mess in Stephen's room and her own and remade the beds with clean sheets.

'I don't know where you get your energy,' she said tiredly as he all but lifted her out of the bath, dried her and pushed her into bed, mumbling something about her being too thin. He handed her a mug of soup and she drank it obediently and then lay down, too tired to argue, and listened to him moving around in the room next door until she fell asleep.

She woke in the middle of the night and tiptoed downstairs to ring the hospital, to find Max there, doing just exactly that. He put the phone down and smiled gently at her.

'He's fine—he's still fast asleep. I'm sorry, did I wake you?'

She shook her head. 'I don't think so. I didn't hear anything.' She laughed self-consciously. 'Sometimes I think we communicate without words.'

'I think we do.' He reached out and took her hands. 'I knew something was wrong the other night. I tried to ignore it, but it wouldn't go away. It was as if you were calling me.'

'I needed you,' she said raggedly. 'I didn't want to, but I—somehow I just couldn't fight it.'

'There's no need to fight it, I'm here,' he murmured.

'Yes, now you are—but for how long?'

He met her eyes, and his own blazed with an emotion she didn't dare to believe. 'For as long as you want me—forever, I hope. I need you, Catherine. I've missed you so much, my life hasn't been worth living. It was only when you and Stephen went away that I realised just how empty my life was. I love you—both of you. Catherine, come back to me. I can't live without you.'

She pulled away, confused and distrustful, afraid to believe him. 'I need commitment, Max, you know that.'

'I'm offering you commitment. I'm offering you my head on a silver platter if that's what you want, but I did have in mind the more normal avenue of marriage.'

She turned slowly, looking up at him in disbelief. 'Marriage?' she said soundlessly.

'Marriage — if you'll have me.'

But it wasn't all over yet.

'What about my job?'

He shrugged expressively. 'I don't know. We haven't got a replacement yet, but I'm still not sure how you feel about it, really. Put it like this. If you had enough money to buy Stephen all the things you wanted to, would you still want to work?'

She thought for a moment, then nodded, aware that she was throwing away her chance of happiness but unable to deny her real self. 'Yes, I would. Not full-time maybe while he's still so young, but yes, I would.'

'And if you had another child?'

Her eyes widened. 'Another child? But I thought you didn't want a child?'

He gave a sad little smile. 'So did I. When you told me you weren't pregnant it hit me like a ton of bricks. I hadn't even realised till then.'

She wasn't aware of the wistful quality of her voice. 'I'd love another baby — perhaps two? Stephen would be thrilled, he's always on about it.'

'And would you want to work?'

She thought about the times she had had to leave Stephen, of the things she had missed and the time that would never be theirs again, and shook her head. 'No. If it wasn't necesssary, no, not for a while. Later, perhaps, when they were all older, then maybe.' She met his eyes searchingly. 'Max, why is it so important to you?'

He shrugged. 'My mother was never at home when I wanted her — always out fundraising or at some charity

lunch or WI coffee morning or something.' His voice
was bleak, and her heart went out to him. 'I was raised
by a succession of nannies, and trotted out periodically
to fly the family flag. I always swore that if I had
children they'd be brought up by a mother who not
only loved them but was there for them.'

'Poor Max.' Cathy lifted her hands and cradled his
cheeks, coming up on tiptoe to lay a kiss on his lips.

'Catherine, just answer my question,' he pleaded.

'I have,' she said, surprised. 'No, I don't think I
would want to work if I didn't have to——'

'Not that one, the other one,' he groaned. 'Will you
marry me?'

'Oh, that one. . .' She grinned mischievously. 'Well,
now, let me see—can you keep me in the style to which
I'd like to become accustomed? Tell me, Dr
Armstrong, what are your prospects——? Oh!'

His arms swept under her and hooked her up against
his chest. 'Just at the moment,' he growled, 'my
prospects of being locked up for murder are very high.
Now, will you or will you not marry me, you aggravat-
ing wench?'

She batted her lashes at him. 'Oh—OK, then, since
you put it so charmingly. How can I resist?'

He released her slowly, sliding her down his body,
and turned her into his arms. His eyes suddenly intent,
he lowered his head and claimed her lips in a searing
kiss that left her knees weak and her heart racing.

'Just to take away any last vestige of resistance,' he
said with a lazy smile.

'There is no resistance. I don't think there ever was.
I love you, Max,' she murmured softly. 'Joan was
right—you're just what the doctor ordered.'

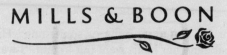

Proudly present to you...

BETTY NEELS' 100TH ROMANCE

Betty has been writing for Mills & Boon Romances for over 20 years. She began once she had retired from her job as a Ward Sister. She is married to a Dutchman and spent many years in Holland. Both her experiences as a nurse and her knowledge and love of Holland feature in many of her novels.

Her latest romance *'AT ODDS WITH LOVE'* is available from August 1993, price £1.80.

— *MEDICAL* *ROMANCE* —

The books for enjoyment this month are:

JUST WHAT THE DOCTOR ORDERED Caroline Anderson
LABOUR OF LOVE Janet Ferguson
THE FAITHFUL TYPE Elizabeth Harrison
A CERTAIN HUNGER Stella Whitelaw

♥ ♥ ♥ ♥ ♥

Treats in store!

Watch next month for the following absorbing stories:

THE STORM AND THE PASSION Jenny Ashe
SOMEBODY TO LOVE Laura MacDonald
TO DREAM NO MORE Patricia Robertson
VET IN POWER Carol Wood

Available from W.H. Smith, John Menzies, Martins, Forbuoys, most supermarkets and other paperback stockists.

Also available from Mills & Boon Reader Service, Freepost, P.O. Box 236, Thornton Road, Croydon, Surrey CR9 9EL.

Readers in South Africa - write to:
Book Services International Ltd, P.O. Box 41654, Craighall, Transvaal 2024.